# *Motion*

H. G. Wells Short Story Competition 2023

Also in this series

# *Motion*

Edited by
Liz Joyce & Tony Scofield

*St Ursin Press*

First published in Great Britain in 2023
by St Ursin Press, 3 Broadfield Court,
1-3 Broadfield Road, Folkestone, Kent CT20 2JT,
United Kingdom

**Sponsors**

ISBN 978-1-7384026-0-1
St Ursin Press is an imprint of Trencavel Press
www.trencavel.co.uk/St Ursin.html

# Contents

## 2023 Senior Prize

# Foreword

One hundred years ago H G Wells published another of his utopian novels entitled *Men Like Gods*. He wrote about a utopian world whose five principles were privacy, free movement, unlimited knowledge, truthfulness, and free discussion. They were all principles widely explored by him in previous works. However he was by then a highly influential figure, both in literary and political circles. He was in 1923 even running for parliament in the London University constituency. He was unsuccessful in the latter and considered himself unsuccessful in the former when he later said of the novel, "It did not horrify or frighten, was not much of a success, and by that time, I had tired of talking in playful parables to a world engaged in destroying itself." The novel was highly influential nonetheless. His utopia was a kind of 'motion' in a debate which his time travelling protagonist from 1921 finds himself embroiled in.

This year's H G Wells Short Story Competition theme of 'Motion' was a rich and diverse one yet oddly enough not a single entry took this meaning of the word. However, entries did abound in reflection of a world in crisis and were not shy of engaging in the debates of our day. This is an English language competition and perhaps Wells would have been well pleased by the cultural diversity that a digital world can deliver.

The H G Wells Short Story Competition was the brainchild of Reginald Turnill who reported on all the Apollo Space missions for the BBC. He lived like Wells, in Sandgate. In a digital world geography can sometimes define us less than common interest and stories have poured in from all over the world across the ether of the internet. Digital technology also allows us to review the entries blindly. Unlike so many competitions, the judges of this one have no idea who the authors are until the winning entries are chosen. The entries carry the hallmark of the time we live in and so it is unsurprising that much of the humour is dystopian.

We are delighted to offer this year's anthology. Many congratulations to those who were shortlisted and to those of you who knew you wrote something excellent just short of an increasingly demanding mark. Writing is an art which does not always offer success. Not much in this world is ideal but we can strive towards it again and again.

CHARLES BAIN SMITH RIBA CA
Chair of Judges

---

# *Ladies' Compartment*

"A. B. C. D! A. B. C. D! 1. 2. 3. 4! 1. 2. 3. 4! 100 'A's and 100 'Z's, your child can count all of these!"

"A. B. C. D! A. B. C. D! 1. 2. 3. 4! 1. 2. 3. 4! 100 'A's and 100 'Z's. Your child can count all of these!"

Ladies' compartment. Train no. 33801. April. 41 degrees Celsius.

Exactly eight stations and 45 minutes after boarding the train, when sweat and irritation had finally blurred its distinctions to seep in and out of my skin, a kind, limping woman gave up the window seat minutes before her destination had arrived—mostly to make her way through an array of sweaty gentlewomen of all sizes and to make sure of her ability of squeezing out of the train when she must.

"A. B. C. D! A. B. C. D! 1. 2. 3. 4! 1. 2. 3. 4! 100 'A's and 100 'Z's. Your child can count all of these!"

"COLD WATER. CO-O-O-LD WATER. ONLY Rs10! ONLY Rs10! ICY HIMALAYAN 10! ONLY Rs10!"

"Girl, can you scooch over a little?" A middle-aged, fair, plump woman asked me as soon as I conquered the newly deserted throne right beside the window. She was sitting on the third seat to my right. I felt hesitant to talk to her; in fact, I specifically waited an extra 10 minutes to get this seat over the one that was being made available to me, right next to that lady—who had been sweating so profusely that I could easily spot her sweat oozing drop by drop on her arms, straight from her temple. From the moment I saw her, there hadn't been any five minute intervals when she hadn't been involved in ill-founded quarrels.

"There's barely any space here, ma'am," I retorted quite quickly but politely.

Unable to please her with my reply, I smiled at her in a vain hope of keeping my civility in its place. The lady on the other hand made a face so displeased that I almost mistook her for feeling constipated. Putting the unused green handkerchief back in her handbag, I saw her complaining to the old lady standing right in front of me, where I had stood for the past 45 minutes:

"See, this young generation! They would study a lot but never learn to respect their elders." Fixing her eyes on me she blurted out sarcastically, "Ma'am!? I don't understand why every Indian is learning their ABCDs! So desperately they want to be 'English', but never respect their own culture. Why don't you address people in your mother tongue, girl?"

I did not intend to continue talking to her. Just a few stations ago I had noticed her argument with another woman who addressed her as 'aunty' in her mother tongue, adhering to the Indian code of respect, but this lady made a similar ruckus with contradicting points of view. To avoid it particularly, I thought 'Ma'am' would have been the most appropriate word to her liking, but alas, you can never please the one who wants to be troubled.

The bookseller who had been trying to sell toddlers' learning books, suddenly hissed at her, "Why are you insulting my trade, Aunty?"

Instantly, a civil war started in the compartment: the two parties shouting at each other, their volume increasing rapidly every second.

*"Who are you calling 'Aunty'?"*

*"You look twice my age, old fool."*

*"She called you 'Ma'am'; you don't like it. I call you 'Aunty'. You don't accept it. What should we call you, Queen Victoria?"*

*"Call your mother that, rascal."*

*"Don't you bring my mother into this, Woman!"*

"SWEET ORANGES. ORANGES SWEET AS HONEY. TELL ME IT'S SOUR AND TAKE BACK YOUR MONEY. THREE ORANGES FOR Rs20. 20! 20! 20!"

*"Of course, I would bring your mother into this. She should have taught you how to respect elders."*

*"You just said I look twice your age! What's..."*

*"Read the books you are selling. You need it more."*
*"I'll give you one for free, Aunty. You read it at home."*

"COLD WATER. CO-O-O-LD WATER. ONLY Rs0! ONLY Rs10! ICY HIMALAYAN 10! ONLY Rs10!"

She got off at the next station. The train started moving again. Strangely enough, I spotted a white woman in the next alley, getting traumatised with the heat and the humongous crowd, neither exclusive of each other. It certainly had been one peculiar experience for her. I wanted to help her. For a second I even considered giving her my window seat, but the sudden gust of wind, although warm, made me quite selfish. Guilt did not let me look at her. If I could, I would have given her some tips to survive the journey in an Indian Local Train.

In fact, if any unfortunate foreigner or an upper middle class Indian with no prior experience had to consider a local train as their means of travel—specially on a hot weekday's office hour—then they must keep these unofficial, unwritten rules in mind:

1. Men, you cannot board on those two specific compartments dedicated to Ladies, unless you want to sell something.
2. You can travel without tickets, but you have to blend in the always moving crowd. Trust me, in twenty years of my life I was never asked for a ticket.
3. Now, you might see alleys in every compartment and in each of those alleys, three seats face three others. Don't be fooled. You have to fit four people on each side, irrespective of body sizes. Four people must sit in the three designated seats.
4. However, if you plan to talk to your partner and let them take the seat in front of you, you will be making the gravest mistake of your life. The alleys, though not meant to be, would be filled with another three or four people, making a human wall between you and your partner.
5. Carry headphones. If you feel like reading, don't. Chances of your book getting damaged by a dozen threats is higher than you securing a peaceful seat for your journey. Plus, your headphones might be able to save you from the continuous shouting and howling of twenty hawkers who sell everything

from food to safety pins. Moreover, it is the slickest way of avoiding conversations. Whether you know anyone on the train or not wouldn't matter as long as you are among the passengers, you are likely to be made a part of the conversations, at all times.

6. Last, but not the least, don't forget to ask the blessed travellers—those who were able to get a seat before you— where they would be getting off so you can secure a deal and take their place in this ever-moving vessel of everyday life.

The old woman sleeping next to me had a visible hunchback even as she was sitting down. Her capabilities to achieve the unthinkable should always remain unquestioned. Patriarchy can claim a thousand things, but if a woman can sleep in a boiling compartment filled with over two hundred sweating human beings howling as if the apocalypse was just a station away, I believe she can even overpower any ferocious man's most torturous subjugation with ease.

As the train approached the next station, she jumped out of her seat, startling every single soul in the alley, seated or not. Seconds after the sporty leap, she caught hold of her bag and started fidgeting to find her cane, which by then had fallen on the dirty floor of the ever-moving vehicle. When I bent down to pick up her cane, I could sense the lady in front of me showing intense irritation with the prospect of her slightly moving, so much so that her 'Tch Tch' distinctly made itself heard among all the commotion and repeated hustles of hawkers selling their voice and commodities all at the same time.

"Is it *Sealdah*?" she asked me as she fixed her worn out glasses in a hurry, while I returned the cane to its fair owner.

"COLD WATER. CO-O-O-LD WATER. ONLY Rs10! ONLY Rs10! ICY HIMALAYAN 10! ONLY Rs10!"

All the women who were initially startled now broke into a deafening laughter.

Before I could tell her, one of the women from the other side of the human wall chuckled, "But this train started from Sealdah station na!" Her high-pitched chuckle really made me curious to have a look at her, but that seemed like an impossible task.

The small old woman slapped her forehead thrice and bit her

tongue, then settling back into her seat started explaining with a tinge of concern, "I am getting so delirious lately."

The high-pitched woman asked her something in reply, but I did not pay attention to their conversation anymore, rather I wanted to find the white woman lost in the crowd, and I indeed made myself a little busy looking here and there for her, but shortly I understood, it wouldn't be much of a success unless I stood up from my seat, which I didn't do after all.

"SWEET ORANGES. ORANGES SWEET AS HONEY. TELL ME IT'S SOUR AND TAKE BACK YOUR MONEY. THREE ORANGES FOR Rs20. 20! 20! 20!"

"My son is in America; he sends me money every month," the old woman proudly said. I looked at her. Her clothes were very cheap. The bag she carried had little holes. I did not believe a word. Other women started enquiring—with the same level of disbelief as I had—what sort of work he did, how good was the paycheck, if he could eat the bad food there, if he had any household helpers or servants there.

"Servants!? Listen to this woman! Those countries don't have any servants, everyone has to do all of the housework, from making food to washing dishes, to cleaning clothes. Everything."

While some women agreed with her, a few others were shocked, mostly because they couldn't imagine a man cleaning clothes and washing dishes. I did not participate or make any contribution to their conversation; I remained a silent listener who was also getting used to the hawkers' cacophonies and hence could tune out of it to listen to women talks.

One among the human walls giggled as she rubbed off sweat from her temple, and then very innocently suggested, "If you had told me, I would have gone with your son, old woman. The family I work for does not even give me enough salary. Every time I ask for a raise, they mention thirty different people that can replace me. I would rather go to a foreign land where there are not many servants available. What do you say?"

She seemed extremely malnourished and terribly young. The bright red vermilion on her scalp made me shudder thinking how that likely early teen was not only married but had been thinking of such worldly things and earning her bread.

Someone from the other side of the wall—almost as if she sat beside the high-pitched woman—hoarsely commented how she cannot afford a flight ticket in the next twenty years. By the time she might get a hold of the ticket, her broken health with all these years of hard labour would make her bed-ridden. The hoarse voice slowly got up from her seat and dictated, "Instead of daydreaming, try to save as much money as possible while you can. Or you might curse yourself as I do right now."

As she started steering herself out of the ocean of people, I could hear her faintly audible murmurs, "Could not even afford medicine for my husband." "No hospital would take him." "Died like a fish taken out of water."

The giggling house-helper did not smile any longer. Seeing her lose the radiance, a young widow on the fourth seat of my side, twisted her lips, "Don't listen to these strangers. No matter what you do, or how much money you have, you cannot keep those who are fated to be departed." Her voice cracked as she said the last word, but she still went on to say, "I don't even cry anymore."

I stared at her, but she kept her gaze fixated on the house-helper. The latter stared past the widow. "If I can live in memory and be happy, what is wrong with your daydream? Don't let these gossiping women on the trains bring you down."

The house-helper flashed a really weak smile and went on to stare at the direction of the window.

A whole new wave of people swarmed in as the train stopped in another junction station, and with it came a tea seller.

"HOT TEA! H-O-T TEA! RAW TEA. GINGER TEA. LEMON TEA. HOT TEA! H-O-T TEA!"

Most likely to lighten the grave mood everyone found themselves in, they started talking among themselves. The old woman beside me suddenly asked the tea seller to come to her alley. After a struggle of three minutes, he could finally squish himself in to serve my neighbouring passenger, who yet again proved herself to be a superhuman, simply by enjoying a cup of hot tea in 41 degrees Celsius.

"Give me a cup of lemon tea, but don't put too much lemon in it."

The tea-seller grunted and asked for Rs10 as he handed her the cup. She took out ten 1-rupee coins and counted them thrice so as not to mistake the amount. Everyone started taunting her, "Oh old woman, your American son should send you 10 rupee notes from next time."

Irritation clouded on her face quite instantly and she finished her tea as fast as she could. Then crumbling the paper cup with all her force, she threw it under her seat. The house -helper suddenly yelled at her for splashing a few drops on her clothes, her innocence long gone, as if she had become a whole different person by then.

The old woman was about to yell back but she suddenly startled everyone yet again by jumping out of her seat and asking me, "Did we leave *Habra* station behind?"

"Yes, the last junction was *Habr...*" Before I could finish my station, she darted off to the gate, which was plausibly the most crowded place of all. When she almost made her way to the gate, the house-helper again found her innocent voice back, "That old woman left her purse back here." Everyone exclaimed how unfortunate it was, some joked about how her son from America can get her a new purse so easily, some tried to call her but it never reached her.

I felt a pang of guilt out of the blue. I took her purse and struggled to get outside. By the time I reached the gate, I could see her walking fast on the platform. I was left with no choice, so I got off and started chasing her. Only when the train had left, I could catch up to her, and hand it over. She blessed me a thousand times, and at a certain point I was sure she was going to cry.

I asked her, "Do you know how to get the train to *Habra*?"

She nodded and pointed towards platform 1 on the other side of the overbridge. I kept looking at her till she crossed it and waited for her train, sitting on a bench under the platform shed. I could see her face glistening with sweat under sunlight. It did not disgust me. She looked helpless and lonely. I wanted to wait for her to get on her train, but as soon as my train arrived, I hesitated for half a second, but then got on my train, the crowd equally suffocating as the train I was on before. I couldn't even get to see the window, seeing the old woman past the window was a far cry; all I could perceive was the same bookseller, trying to sell his toddlers' learning book in another Ladies' Compartment.

"A. B. C. D! A. B. C. D! 1. 2. 3. 4! 1. 2. 3. 4! 100 'A's and 100 'Z's. Your child can count all of these!"

"A. B. C. D! A. B. C. D! 1. 2. 3. 4! 1. 2. 3. 4! 100 'A's and 100 'Z's. Your child can count all of these!"

## *Cast Out of Heaven*

I woke up with a jolt, tears tracing their intricate paths precariously down my flushed cheeks onto the damp pillow.

I hastily flicked them away and headed to the mirror. Red-rimmed eyes stared back, empty and haggard. Soulless.

Heaving heavily, I retched into the sink, expelling the bitter bile, until what remained behind was the barest hint of a foul aftertaste. I could hear the taunting echoes of my father's ghost, sending ripples and distorting my already turbulent headspace. *Stop crying. Dignified Chinese men don't cry.*

Then why won't the tears stop?

I flopped down on my seat, cane heedlessly disposed on the side, fully aware of the repercussions that followed. Of course I was assigned this seat for convenience. I loathed the teachers for skirting around the elephant in the room during our discussions, offering oh-so-delicate niceties, pity dripping off their voices like viscous honey. For me or them, that's the question.

No one took any notice of me. My classmates were engrossed in copying off others' homework, gushing over the tours of their beloved idols, or having an impromptu match of catch-the-schoolbag. Not that I cared. It was always better than the false sympathies showered needlessly on me. The news about my plight would garner no more attention, now that everyone had heard of at least a dozen versions of it. Typical Hong Kong behaviour. Stories rapidly expired, replaced by fresh exhilarating scoops, something better, something grander, something more outrageous.

It is a household myth that a goldfish has a memory of seven seconds. Apparently, the memory of human beings could be even shorter.

A firm hand slammed onto my desk, snapping me out of my reverie. My eyes flicked up and I found myself staring into the effervescent look on Michael's face.

"Sup, Mick?"

"Luce, buddy, lighten up!" He teased, eyes twinkling. His hand reached out to ruffle my slick hair, and I yanked out my textbook to hit him square in the face. He smirked at my aggression, emotion and life bleeding out of him. I was like that too. Until the unspeakable occurred.

"Mick, cut to the chase. I'm in no mood for your silly games." I put him off reflexly, his efforts of cheering me up falling flat as eggs against a brick wall.

"Fine," he sighed, shoulder drooping in hyperbolic disappointment. Ever the drama queen. "Listen, are you free this Saturday? The Royal Ballet from London is in town. Angelica can help us get top seats! It'll be just like the old times." He gushed, an onslaught of words spewing out from the sliver of gaps in his reservoir.

I froze up like a deer in the headlights. Michael winced, knowing that he had hit a sore spot.

"I got a physiotherapy session." I brushed him off nonchalantly, struggling to keep the wavering out of my voice. I couldn't continue and I knew it. If I headed past the point of no return, I'm sure to lose composure. The prickling wetness was gathering in my eyes, and it took all my effort to stop blinking, lest the droplets dripped out.

"But..." Michael tried, but I raised my hand as if to stop the words from flowing out of him. Taping the bandage onto the wound.

My wound. The one that was sore and festering around the edges of my heart. My leg gave a shot of phantom pain in its chrysalis, reminding me of my predicament.

Michael gave me another pleading look, but I stood firm. Warm chocolate eyes clashed against cold dark ones, his passionate fire against my icy unyielding demeanour. I pushed bit by bit until he finally caved in with a resigned exhale.

"If you're sure about that, Lucifer. We won't push, but talk to Angelica, will you? She's chill, but even now she's getting worried."

"Yeah, sure, Michael," I answered, my eyes already wandering to the azure peeking behind the window. But I was not ready to face Angelica yet. Here's the thing about the fast-paced city of Hong Kong—they expect you to breeze through obstacles, to move forward swiftly, to adapt rapidly, so as not to be caught up with the opposing tide. But they didn't seem to realise the gravity of my situation, how traumatising it was to have your dreams ripped off from your grasp in a fraction of a second. There's nothing malicious about their intent, but it continued to frustrate me to no end.

Sparing a final forlorn glance my way, Michael trudged back to his classroom, waiting for the telltale ring of the bell to start our everyday routine. Time rolls in a wheel, ripping reality out of our greedy clutches, pushing us to look at the future, radiant and glimmering, ahead.

That's what people do. They move on.

And what's left was the scalded palms of a teenage boy, desperately clinging to the past. Pushing his weight onto the wheel, he pleads for the motion to halt, perhaps just for a second.

It never came.

"Mommy! Look!" A bright-eyed kid tugged anxiously at his mother's sleeve, fighting to grab her attention from the phone.

The mother glanced up from her screen and inspected the bright tutu with narrowed eyes saturated with slight but undisguised disdain. "Sweetie, that's inappropriate for you. I'll find you something that I guarantee you will like—perhaps soccer?"

"No! The other boys are mean," he whined. "Jason tripped me. I don't wanna go there anymore."

The woman huffed, clearly frustrated with the conversation. "Lucifer, no. Ballet is a feminine sport. Perhaps you would find your calling in basketball? Jeffrey seems to enjoy it."

However, there was no swaying of the little kid's mind. In retrospect, the mother should have anticipated the inevitable tantrums. After six smashed dishes, three uneaten dinners, and a dozen screaming arguments, the mother finally caved in.

"Alright, little man. You got what you want. Happy?" She groaned in exasperation as the quixotic boy rewarded her with a toothy grin. She mentally slapped her forehead against the wall. "At least it'll look good in his portfolio, right?"

Mother might have thought my love for ballet was a fling. She would have never thought that I would fall in love with the steady rhythm of the art, the familiar sting during splits, nor the exhilarating feeling of soaring when I leaped across the dance floor.

One thing that I adore about ballet is the fluidity of the motion. Everything was of calculated perfection, always flowing, always graceful, always elegant. A work of art at its finest. Every arabesque, every glissade, every jeté reminded me how brightly a fire glowed. There was never a dull moment, and everything was constantly moving, improvising to create something novel.

It was not to say that my road in ballet was smooth sailing. I could still hear hushed whispers of my parents, wanting me to devote more time to my studies and fretting over the fact that I might be gay. "Danseurs are gay." My dad proclaimed *ad nauseam*, like a mantra, staring into my eyes with disgust, as if wishing to squish a disgusting cockroach within. To him, being gay was one of the gravest sins I could commit, the first one being dead.

I might not be gay, but in their eyes, I'm already disowned. I'm not the perfect son, the one that was traditionally masculine, nor the one that would be a doctor someday, affluent and prosperous.

Slight snickers from my classmates were no help either. Teasing was usually subtle, backhanded compliments were commonplace, and I had the word 'pervert' scribbled on my table more than once. The pencil stains were a pain to remove, and often my hands were smuggled by the abundant graphite from rubbing the smudges all afternoon.

All the opposition should be reason enough to quit. Not for the headstrong boy. In the studio, I could fully express myself, letting the pent-up energy flow out of me to my legs, trusting them to catch me every time. Ballet was where I was free, allowing me to be swept away by the melodious tunes and the intricate motion of my physique. It was my heaven, and free I was.

The ringing of the bells snapped me out of my line of thought. I flung my school bag onto my shoulder, picked up my cane, and walked out of the corridor, wincing at every limp. Running down the halls was unimaginable, and I was imprisoned in this lowly flesh, struggling with every step.

I trudged on, thankful that at least I was able to walk. The past few months were torture, my useless ankle had left me hopping on another with my crutches. At least I got off the cast, I reassured myself. But it's a far cry from being completely fine. I had to take at least a few brief rests between school and the bus station when the sudden pangs of pain attacked me. During these impromptu stops, I stood motionless, my chest heaving while waves and waves of faceless people rolled by. From time to time I felt like a battered fish, staring at the shoal of vibrant ribbons skimming by, scales gleaming under the bright sunlight.

The world was turning, but I was not.

I felt a drip of wetness on my head, followed by a few more in quick succession. Darn it, I forgot to bring an umbrella. I tried to walk faster, knowing the telltale signs of a giant downpour, sighing as more droplets attacked my hair, my face, and my eyes. My vision blurred, and god knows whether it was from the rain or tears that I struggled to hold in. Messy tendrils of hair framed my face, escaping the cold confinement of the gel, and leaving me shivering and dishevelled.

Raising my head to the darkened skies, I silently voiced a question: 'Dear raindrops, do you hurt when you fall out of heaven?'

"It is decided! Our leading lady for Swan Lake would be Angelica Chan, and her understudy would be Gabriella Lee. For our gents..." I held my breath, my heart hammering in trepidation, threatening to burst out any second. "Prince Siegfried would be portrayed by Lucifer Lau, and his understudy would be Michael Yau. You are now dismissed."

Compliments from my teammates erupted and I accepted them graciously, but I could not resist the hints of a proud beam creeping up my cheeks. Being the lead would open a huge door of opportunities. Our trio was approaching our final year, and a production of this scale would attract talent and university scouts like bees to honey. Perhaps they would be impressed with our performance and give us the scholarships necessary to pursue this passion and further elevate our art.

After all, my parents weren't my staunchest supporters. My sore throat reminded me of that.

At last, I turned to Michael with a huge beam on my face. He smirked back and extended his hand for a handshake. Truce. "Good job, bro."

I caught his hand and teasingly placed a kiss on the back of his hand. "Same to you, Michael. I look forward to our eventual partnership," I replied, my tone saturated with mock formality.

He jerked his hand back. "Save your kisses for Angelica!" he admonished lightly.

"Hey! We're all friends, that's all."

"Uh-huh." He nodded unconvincingly. "You two make a dashing couple, by the way."

I was about to retort when I heard the familiar lilt of a mellifluous voice behind me. "Congratulations, Luce. I knew it would be either one of you. Drinks for celebration?"

"Sure!" I agreed enthusiastically, knowing full well that the drinks entailed were probably freezing lemon tea from the nearest vending machine. Shame that there's no tolerance for underage drinking. Not wanting to be a killjoy, I yelled: "Race you to the bus stop! Loser buys the drinks!" holding in my mirth as Angelica gave an indignant squawk. "Not fair! Your legs are longer than mine!"

I shrugged and turned to Michael. "Buddy, do you agree with this race?"

Michael grinned, a competitive glint in his eyes. "Be careful, I might beat you in this one."

"Game on."

Minutes later, pedestrians would note the three teenagers bursting out of the studio, running against the flow of people, narrowly dodging elderlies and yelling apologies on the way, their raucous laughter melting as one part of the hustle and bustle of Hong Kong. A familiar crack on my shoulders resonated in my head. I winced as I slowly rolled my shoulders, trying to alleviate the tension on my back. A glance at Angelica told me that she wasn't faring any better. Locks of dark hair were starting to spill out from her messy bun, and her face was flushed with fatigue and exertion.

"Again," came the voice of steel from Madame Chung. We started to open our mouths in protest, but she silenced us with a glare. "We'll start from the beginning. Nah-nah, no complaints. We're slightly behind schedule, and the technique needs to be perfect."

I took a deep breath and steadied myself. Saltiness had become a constant companion on my tongue, and my arms ached with hours of lifting and spinning. Being a lead in a major production had taken a toll on my muscles. Daily practices and technique refinement caused a steep learning curve, and more time devoted to ballet means less time to study and sleep, and more conflicts with my parents. But when the familiar notes of the *Swan Lake* ballet suite filtered through the loudspeaker, I snapped into position, ignoring the twang of pain on my heel. Probably nothing but a sprain, I reasoned. Nothing major. Don't be something serious. I could not afford that.

However, as I spun in time with the music, the vice on my neck winding tighter and tighter, I was left wondering what would be the straw that breaks the camel's back.

Bright lights shone onto the stage. Backstage, I stared mesmerised by Angelica in her black swan outfit. She was dancing Odile's solo, looking ever so enchanting, the ebony feathers on her skirt shiny and pristine, the sequins glittering under the spotlight. Dancing with energy, her motions were clean and fluid, and there was never a hint of waver or hesitation in her steps. I saw her nail every *pas de chat* and *cabriole* with precision, oozing with confidence and charm, fleshing out the seductiveness and slyness of Odile. Gone was my demure friend Angelica, and in her place was Odile in all her glory, flaunting her victory in the face of poor Odette.

It was approaching the end of her solo. Time for the trickiest part of the whole show—the Black Swan *pas de deux*. I steeled myself and ran my fingers on my slick-back hair for one last time, allowing the persona of a smitten prince to wash over me. An electrifying tingle travelled from my core to my limbs, anticipating the time that they would be unbridled again. My parents and future are watching, I chide myself. Give your best shot.

As I stepped forward to the centre of the platform, I felt another pang on my bad ankle and barely resisted the urge to massage it. Focus: there are better things to worry about.

I stepped onto the stage, temporarily blinded by the spotlight, before giving my most charismatic smile to the audience. Turning to Angelica, I opened my right arm towards her in invitation, and she gladly took it.

We danced, our muscle memories merging as we delivered our best. I tried to hide my winces when we turned in synchrony, earning a slight narrowing of eyes and tilting of the head from my partner. I shook my head subtly, and turned to the crowd, flashing another beam.

She turned away, unconvinced. The piece was building up to a crescendo, and it was time for one of the most technically challenging steps: the *fouettés en tournant*.

Angelica spun forward. I saw her briefly focusing before starting her turns. Round and round she spun like a top, matching the rhythm of the tune. Thirty, thirty-one, thirty-two. She stopped twisting and grinned widely, welcoming the thunderous applause.

Mentally bracing for the oncoming torture of my limb, I steeled myself. Good thing that I only needed to perform eight. My leg wobbled at the second spin but I shouldered on.

I'm almost there. The music blaring at its climax couldn't cover the booming of blood pounding against my ears. One more, one more, the last one—

An audible snap echoed through the hall. An excruciating fire burnt at my right ankle, dashing any thought of plantarflexing it again. I yelped as I stumbled onto the wooden floor, my arms outstretched to brace myself from the impact.

I saw a quick flurry of dark feathers and found myself staring at the eyes of Angelica blown wide in concern. Then I noticed the flock of swans behind her, staring at us with beady eyes, craning their necks to get a better view. Their gaze was sharp and accusing, blaming me for everything that happened to their beloved princess. Your fault, it hissed vehemently. Your flaw.

I couldn't take it anymore. Brushing away Angelica's outstretched hand, I hopped backstage, hanging my head in shame. Prince Siegfried was long gone, and what was left was the hollow husk of Lucifer Lau. I fell, and I failed.

My fault.

Michael was the first to rush to me. "Lucifer!"

I refused to look at him, already stripping my costume off. Michael caught my hand, and I pushed him away. "Seems that I would not be dancing as Prince Siegfried tonight, huh?" I snarked, venomous sarcasm encasing every word.

Angelica stepped forward, trying to comfort me, but I drew away. "Leave. You got a show running on, Miss prima ballerina."

I regretted it as soon as the words left my mouth, but I couldn't bring myself to apologise, not with the vortex of fury and disappointment swirling tumultuously inside me. Angelica's wounded look was enough to make me feel guilty, and I knew that it would leave a dark stain on my conscience.

I had never snapped at them. Now I did, but I could not bring myself to care.

Madame Chung rushed in with a chair, escorting me to it. I had to credit Madame for it, she was an efficient machine under stress. "Michael, get changed and prepared for Act 4. Angelica, change to Odette. The sudden intermission would be fifteen minutes, so there's no time to waste. The show must go on!"

Sparing a parting glance, they rushed off. Michael was instantly caught under the fury of make-up artists and hairdressers, all clambering to turn him into the ravishing prince. Under normal circumstances, I would have teased him. But I couldn't find it in myself to smile.

"Lucifer, I got some ice for you. You better have your leg checked after the performance. Do I need to call the ambulance?" Muttering my thanks, I practised basic first aid on my injury but refused the offer of an ambulance ride. The last thing I would need was for my friends to see me being carted away in a wheelchair.

In no time, the show resumed. Michael, now as Seigfried, was reeling at Odile's deception, and Angelica, as Odette, was heartbroken at Seigfreid's betrayal. Eyes glued to the stage, I watched as they flew across the theatre, the brightness of Angelica's tutu reminding me of an angel's wings rather than a swan. She looked seraphic, the traces of evil long gone, and what was left was pure love, adoration, and tender forgiveness. They glided along the floor, portraying the story with their bodies until their deaths, bodies entwined into one.

They were made for this, I thought bitterly. The cast straight out of heaven. Perfect for the art, perfect for each other.

Never tearing my eyes off them, I mentally vocalised a question: 'How did Lucifer feel when he looked up in the sky to his past residence, staring at the fluffy clouds and the cheery angels laughing so merrily, as he rotted at the dark inferno beneath the earth?'

Guess I would find out soon.

Squinting at the blurred monochrome film, I turned to the doctor, fidgeting slightly.

"A complete tear in the Achilles tendon and slight fracturing in the lateral malleolus of the fibula is found. We would need to put on a cast for it to heal properly. Don't put pressure on your right ankle for at least a couple of months, and physiotherapy would take place two weeks later. Meanwhile..." came the monotonous verdict. Judging at the listless look of the doctor, this was not his first patient in breaking bad news. To him, I was just another face in the rapid tide of nameless men, but to me, his callous apathy was a stab in the heart.

"At least a couple of months? How about ballet?" Try as I could, the quiver in my voice was audible even in my ears.

"I'm sorry, but you need to put that on hold for at least six months. If you overexert it you risk further damage and the ankle might have a reduced angle of motility. The best thing you can do is rest." Eyeing my despondent expression, his tone softened. "You're a student, right? Perhaps it's time to focus more on your studies and get into a good university."

I was silent when my parents wheeled me out of the room, ready for the reprimand that ensued.

It was my dad who started. "Son, maybe it's a sign. You still have a year to prepare for your public examinations, and you know how cut-throat the competition is. Perhaps it's better if you could stop ballet for this period, and focus on real life."

His words raised the simmer up to a boil. The volcano was set on the trajectory of eruption, and caustic retorts were threatening to splash out from the bubbling cauldron. "Guess you're secretly glad about it, huh?" I answered blithely. "You finally got the son you wanted. A bit damaged, but who cares when I land on a spectacular office job, right? Congratulations." I clapped sardonically, knowing that each clap would aim a blow to my parents' hearts. Anger and disappointment consumed me, and I lashed out blindly, aiming to maim them with every blow.

An angel without his wings. Tumbling down, his descent to earth was clumsy, a mutilated wing spiralling as he tried to cushion the fall. All that was left was a cripple, a stationary object in the world of speed and motion. Forcibly cut off ahead of his prime.

A resonating slap caused my head to forcibly snap to the side. Resisting the urge to cup my stinging cheek, I glared at my father, noting how the flesh on his porky face flushed red with fury.

"I'm your father. How dare you talk to me like that, you ungrateful little brat!" Came the torrent of curse words. We were garnering attention now based on the side glares from the staff and the other patients.

"I didn't ask for you to be my father," I answered curtly. Without sparing another glance, I wheeled myself out, ignoring the choked splutters behind. My further input would only escalate the situation.

Fuming, I phoned Michael. He picked up after the second ring. "How's the leg?" He asked bluntly, straight to the point. So atypical of him.

"Needs months to heal."

A deafening silence ensued. "I'm sorry." He replied, his tone sombre as if in mourning. Injury is often a pernicious blow to a dancer's career. I could bid my opportunities goodbye. Who knows when I could reach my maximum potential again. I need to retrain my muscles, especially my atrophied ankle after months of disuse. Strength training requires time too, time that I did not have to spare.

"Don't be. It's not your fault. At least some of us will get into the Royal Ballet School, right?"

"About that..." came the pregnant pause. "No offence, but Angelica got an invitation to the first-round auditions of the San Francisco Ballet School. She might stand a sporting chance."

"San Francisco Ballet School," I parroted numbly. "Well, good for her." My voice sounded flat even in my ears.

"Luce..."

"Save it." I ended the call abruptly. Irrational jealousy was poisoning my head. Angelica was flawless, I knew that as a fact. But her victories reminded me of what I had lost.

I knew that I was playing with fire, and one day, the flames might devour me whole, leaving behind a trail of soot, dust, and destruction in its wake.

The storm finally came to a stop. I saw the hint of rose and took it as my cue to leave. Mechanically boarding the bus, I headed home, staring at the cars speeding by until they melted into indiscernible blobs of light.

Alighting at my destination, I entered my building and pressed the button for floor 14. Stepping out to the rooftop, I took a second to take in the dusk in its full grandeur. The diaphanous rays were struggling to escape the cosset of the graying clouds. They were fighting the losing battle for the night to come. At last, darkness would take over the world, forcing the other colours out of their glory.

Darkness wins every night. Always.

I sat near the edge of the building, body slumped against the rail with my feet dangling in the air. There's a certain thrill of danger that helps clear my mind. Besides, I needed my solitude. No one would find me here. Elders avoided this place like the plague. Fourteen is inauspicious, they warned. It sounded too much like the words 'must die' in Cantonese. Too many misguided souls around here others cautioned, wrinkling their noses to the ghastly scent of their imaginary ghosts.

I didn't mind. It's peaceful here. No one would judge me, or make any demands. Here's the fine line between life and death. Countless people had stepped over the ledge, crossing the final barrier, the last step of their lives. But I know my time is not up. Not yet.

Below me, there's life. Rubies and emeralds blinked, heralding ants across the traffic. They scuttled, navigating through the streets towards their abode. Tiny vehicles basked in the amber lights which bestowed a safe passage home. There's always the occasional horn and the roar of an engine, a beast awakened from its slumber. A cluster of ongoing activities down there while I stay still.

It's not that I couldn't move on. I didn't want to, knowing that moving on meant accepting my fate, allowing all my past efforts to slip through my fingers and vanquish down the river of time until they become nothing but a fleeting fantasy, a fragment of my imagination.

Absent-mindedly, I played with the puddle left behind by the previous shower. Catching a glimpse of myself, I did a double-take, almost not recognising the reflection. Gone was the lively young man, and in his place was an aged soul with wild unkempt hair burning with melancholy, fury, and resentment—an old man living in the past.

It's my future gone, part of me rationalised. It made me like that.

How about blaming your stubbornness, your rancorous disregard for others who had an ounce of love for you, only for you to reminisce about your halcyon days? Another part of me argued.

I inhaled, my breath weighing down my core. It's too much for a night. As I headed down, I was unaware of the puddle set squarely in front of me.

I slipped, arms flailing as I tumbled back, my blood roaring with adrenaline as I fell back closer to the edge. I caught the glimmer of silver, perhaps the spirits beckoning me to join their charade. Join us in the past, they ghosted. End this life, shackled in lowly mortal flesh. Join us in spirit, as we roam into the deadly nights.

There's only one thought that kept them at bay. My racing heart fuelled by the desire to live. The rushing blood coloured my cheeks, begging me for survival. No, I realised. I don't want to die. Not physically or spiritually.

A piercing clang resonated into the night, and my head impacted painfully onto the rusty rail, my timely defence against death. I peered down and noticed that it would have been a couple of meters of me free-falling to my demise.

Catching my breath, I raised my head towards the darkened canopy. The full moon glowed gloriously in her dappled beauty, banishing the apparitions that seduced me to join their ranks. She cast her precious moonlight to guide me towards the steps of the living, where there was a cosy meal waiting at the table and the rapturous laughter of my best friends welcoming the old Lucifer back.

I could feel the gears of time shift, and for once, I'm not opposing it. I'm freely embracing the opportunities that it would bring.

Granting a luminous smile towards the moon, I headed forward, not glancing back. I was positive that Selene winked.

The boy glanced at his lissom partner, taking in the reassuring nod.

Brandishing his looming thoughts, he allowed his intuition to take control, turning in sync with his partner. She gave a bashful grin as she pranced away lithely, allowing his solo to shine. On and on he spun, the ghost of ballet possessing him, imbuing him with unrivalled passion and gracefulness. At last, he ended with the fifth position, waves of happiness washing through him. He could spot his ardent supporters in the crowd, cheering him on.

He was aware of the curtain of applause as he took his final bow. But all he heard was silence. Peace at last.

GLORIA MESA

## *Rain Dance by Leyelle*

Holding my hands to the sky, I try to dance. And I feel I'm almost free for the only time in forever.

I can feel the wind, the east wind, I think, in the tassels of my hair. I have green beads at the base of the knotty braids as if I'm a palm tree forming its first fruits. In the summertime, I'll change them to red.

I am very small—and stocky—for a palm tree. Stretch as I might, I don't even begin to break into the blue sky. Two fingers blot out the sun when I close one eye. But when I open it, I'm still small. It's still everything. Too powerful to follow my bidding.

My shadow on the wall looks prettier than I do.

It's slimmer and taller, and dark.

All the scars on my face and arms are washed out into one uniform splotch, like a paint splatter thrown against the white.

I only dance when nobody's looking.

One time my older brother caught me and jeered, "Waddle fatty. Ugly duck."

I can move gracefully, I know. The shadow doesn't lie that much.

It dances across the grass in long ghosts, never missing a beat—at least not to the music in my head.

When we grow up, we are going to be farmers.

Nobody tells us, but we still know it's true.

That's what our father was and our mother's father too.

And we sometimes dream of other things, but what can we do?

23

Things stay the same here, not because it's better, but because they've always stayed the same. And in that consistency, we stay constant to the death. We will never change, and we are constant in that.

Even the crops this year are determined to be stagnant. The soil is bad, and our educated college cousins say it's because of the beans.

Growing the same things in the soil year after year wears it down, the same way this sameness is wearing us down.

Still, we need the beans. We need the harvest.

I sing a song to the little sprouts about growing up, though I'm not sure what that means.

I dance with them so they'll know what it means to move and to change.

As the days lengthen, I sing constantly, like a spell, a conjuration, or a plea.

I whisper this song to the walls as well, so my parents will dream of it too.

Late nights, I hear them whisper, there is a storm coming.

Even if it passes over our island, the winds will probably hit us, and all our plantain sepas and beans will be wiped out.

In the city, they all live in houses made of concrete and these houses won't be harmed by the storm.

They go to work in buildings too—and they will still be there after the storm—after the winds if they are all we get.

The winds move faster than we do. They go places we refuse to go.

When the first sign of the storm appeared, it seemed mild. We were sent to school anyway because it wasn't even raining.

I watched the little trees sway in the wind, bending but not breaking.

I watched the big trees snap in the middle.

My father doesn't know how to read. He could learn. The city runs a program for the older generation, giving out school books for free and night lessons, but he never goes.

My mother is trying to learn. She fumbles over the same books my little brothers are reading, and I know she's embarrassed, but she won't quit.

As we study, my father stays locked away in his bedroom. The strong breeze seems to be gathering its strength—practising pushing over our lives. It gradually swells into a gale, forcing the red-faced hibiscus into the earth. For 30 seconds or so, they do nothing but kiss the soil, but they rise again, red-faced, but still beautiful.

Mother asks me to help her sound out a word.

One tree fell on a power line, and the electricity went out for everyone. It won't be fixed until the city sends out its men. No one is going out in weather like this.

Nobody except my father.

My older brother and my father head up the hill to check on the crops. Even though it's windy, they look over every mango as if there's nothing else in the world. They check to see if anything can be harvested now, though they know nothing is even close to ready.

It will all be lost. I'm sure.

Mother and I wait by the front door, rigid with worry, in matching posture, our calloused hands clasped to faded blouses.

Anxiously, we watch my father's face when he comes back inside, but he just snorts at us as if we caused the hurricane.

The rain started around dinner time while we were saying the blessing. Daddy didn't even pause in his sentence.

We all opened our eyes though we shouldn't have and stared toward the window, which has no pane, only a blanket nailed to the wall blocking the opening.

One strong gust and the blanket tore away from the wall, skidding up to my feet, soggy—smelling of mildew.

The next gust of wind blew out the candle.

Mother pinned the blanket back up.

We ate in the dark.

The floor below the window is forming a little pool, one metre by half a metre, but it's spreading.

In the gap between the front door and the concrete floor, there is another puddle, but this one is shimmering.

The orangey shine of the street light is in its middle, and by our door, it is murky and brown. The brown and the orange mix together, dissipating into almost crystal clear at the edges—something like a watercolor sunset—melting into the mountain.

I know the water is a bad sign, but for now, it's beautiful.

Everyone goes to bed when Daddy says to. It's early. 7 p.m.

Mother shoves towels into the space under the door and tacks another over the blanket covering the window.

We lay beneath our mosquito nets, on our slouching mattresses, and watch.

When it's about midnight, I see her light a candle. She takes out her textbook and hunches over it at the table.

In about five seconds, Daddy is leaning over her, telling her to put the light out. We don't know when the storm will end or when the city will fix the electricity.

Mother snuffs out the candle, and Daddy goes to bed, grumbling.

After he falls asleep, she turns on the light on her cracked flip phone.

At 2 a.m., the wind begins screaming.

Everyone is silent, but I don't believe they are sleeping.

It feels as if someone is picking up the house and shaking it. We hear a thousand sounds like woods cracking and branches falling. But nothing falls on us, and the little house stands, somehow.

I tiptoe out of bed onto the bedroom floor that's muddy and damp.

I walk with mincing steps to the front room, haunted by ghosts of the storm that gets in through the cracks and windows. On all sides, I feel them surrounding me, whisking past my damp skin, plummeting into my chest. The night shrieks with melody and horror.

I face the wall.

I can't see my shadow, but I'm sure she's trying to keep breathing, too.

*It's too late to be up and dancing.*

I still hear the wind screaming, but I can't sleep. So I dance.

Now and then, there's a noise that scares me. My heart seems to stop, and my skin grows cold, but I dance on.

*'Anyway. Anyway.'*

The wind won't keep me from being beautiful.

My shadow on the wall is a good partner. She never comments on the steps that I mess up or the times when I'm awkward, tripping over my own feet.

Slowly, I get better. I learn to understand how I move.

I forget the storm as I twirl. One step. Two steps.

*It's too dark to be laughing—dancing.*

I don't care. I dance anyway. I'll always dance.

At about 7 a.m., the storm subsides. All of a sudden, the sky goes from gray to yellow-blue.

It's strange to imagine that the sun was already up behind the clouds. There is no sunrise today. Just darkness and then light. The first day.

Now I go to bed with dirty feet.

Everything is muddy and wet anyway. The floor will have to be mopped, the laundry washed, and the furniture wiped down, too.

But I go to bed, peaceful and content, while my father keeps sleeping, tired and angry.

There will be no waking up early today. Maybe any day, for a long time.

Everything is gone. Destroyed.

The storm washed away the bean plants. It knocked down all the sepas, the guandules, and even some of the mango trees.

My older brother says the storm has passed over the island—it's over now—but it took with it lots of trash, construction debris, and plant waste—and it washed them out into the ocean, to foreign seas.

Maybe some part of our farm is even there now, floating away somewhere exotic.

Daddy doesn't say anything at all. He just stares at the earth without pity, affection, or sadness. He lost everything he had as his forefathers did—and we'll keep doing—every time a storm hits.

He turns quickly now and grabs his boots. There are crops to replant.

And I sit on our front steps, thinking of oceans, the weather, and storms, all things that dance and change—never quite the same thing twice.

# RADIYAH NOUMAN

## *Away the Water Drains*

Aasiya was shivering. Water dripped from her arms and face as she stood ankle-deep on the very edge of the river. She could hear her mother's bangles clinking a few feet away from where she stood. *Ching, ching, ching.*

They sounded lovely, jingling away as her Ami Jan performed her ablution. Aasiya glanced over to where her grandmother stood hunched over with the other women, washing her feet. They were a bit further deep, where little girls weren't allowed due to the strong waves.

A crisp breeze started up again, so cold in the winter months that Aasiya was sure her nose would fall off. She could already see it, blue and black, jumping off and running into the distance. She immediately clamped her hands on it; she couldn't be without a nose. Meanwhile, the water glistened and gushed, unaffected.

"Aasiya *puttar*, if you're done, come inside with me," Dadi Ji called.

The 7-year-old turned and sloshed over to the green shore where her *chappal* had been haphazardly placed. She pulled down the lowers of her *shalwar* from where she had tucked them around her knees and hobbled over to the mud hut. Her grandmother was already feeding more wood to the sputtering flames. Aasiya knelt in front of it, letting the warmth seep in while keeping a close eye on her little sister, Saima, babbling away in a corner of the room. Saima had gotten her grubby hands on Aasiya's favourite toy one time. Never again.

Dadi Ji had spread out the prayer mats in the time that Ami Jan came inside. The three of them stood, adjusting their head scarves before beginning their Friday prayers. Aasiya's head scarf was the best in her opinion. It was a light pink silk with blue flowers embroidered onto it. The cloth had been a gift from her father. He had bought one for each of the girls out of the extra pay he got when the farm earned a profit from the harvest last year. Aasiya's older brother said it was due to 'soil fertility'; he was just eager to show off what he learned in school. Dadi Ji's head scarf was a rich brown with rust-red flowers, while Ami Jan had pink flowers on a lush green. Saima hadn't been born then so she didn't have one yet. Not that she was old enough to care.

They ended their prayers and set about making lunch. Aasiya crouched down, rolling her sleeves as her mother placed a metal dish on the ground. Aasiya set about punching and rolling the mixture of flour and water until it formed a nice dough. She played with it for a bit until her mother scolded her and made her take it outside where Dadi Ji had trapped a little fire in a circle of stones, flat pan already heating up on top of it. The two women, both young and old, separated the dough into twelve smaller pieces, and rolled each of them out between the palms of their hands, nice and thin. Dadi Ji slapped one onto the pan, using her fingers to flip it over once it was cooked through. Aasiya could only watch. Little girls weren't allowed near fires either.

After the rotis were cooked, the women spread out the few dishes they had on the worn-down carpet in the centre of the room. Ami Jan placed the curry in the middle, still in the *karahi* it was cooked in.

"Amma! Ruqqia! We're home!" A familiar male voice called from outside.

"Oh good! I was beginning to worry. Come quick, or the food will get cold. Hassan, take off your shoes. How many times do I have to tell you?!" Ami Jan went full mother hen on her husband and son as they returned from work and school respectively.

Aasiya ran to greet her father, who lifted her into his arms. She grinned at the grunt he let out; she was getting bigger! Saima screeched her head off demanding attention, which was duly given by Aasiya's older brother, Hassan, screaming back at her. Dadi Ji calmly and expertly directed everyone towards the food, murmuring blessings on each of them as she did so.

The Bajwas all sat down to eat with the river's music soothing their ears, playing the same melodies as usual.

Aasiya heaved the bucket out of the river, balancing it on her shoulder as she sloshed her way out of the water. She had to go further in to fill the bucket up, since the edge of the river had dried up over the years. If only it would rain. She liked the rain.

"Ami, here's the water," Aasiya said, turning to her mother.

She was sat on the bare floor, fanning herself with a handmade straw fan made by Hassan. Beads of sweat trickled down her forehead as the scorching July heat made its way in every corner of the house.

"Give me a glassful of it, *beta*. I really cannot stand this heat any longer. Oh God, why do you punish me so?" Ami Jan's lip trembled.

Aasiya simply sighed, feeling quite done with her mother's tantrums. Even she wasn't that moody, and she was at the ripe age of 13. Ami Jan was just making a fuss.

Aasiya trudged off to do the remaining chores after handing her mother some water. She grabbed the dirty laundry along with the soap and made her way back to the glistening river. The rocks that used to be a part of the riverbed were now exposed, smoothed out over the years. She set to scrubbing the clothes with vigour; good exercise to let out all her teenage frustrations. As she washed the clothes and wrung them out, she made sure to splash some water on herself. The sun was blazing down on her, and she could feel her skin melting off.

"Aasiya! Get the food ready, your brother will be back soon. He'll be starving, poor child," Ami Jan called out from the doorway, stroking her round belly for comfort.

The river calmly whispered its secrets to indifferent ears as Aasiya stomped over to the mud hut, crushing the dry grass beneath her. She just wanted to sit down for a bit and fan herself. Frustration rolled off her in waves as she set about chopping and cooking the thick slab of meat that Abu's employer had given them the other day.

"Oi, *chotti*! Make yourself useful for once. Knead this dough," Aasiya harshly yanked Saima into the makeshift kitchen.

The little girl quickly sat down and set to work, sensing her sister's annoyance. However, she couldn't avoid the scolding she got when she started playing with the dough instead. By the time lunch was ready Dadi Ji was hobbling back from visiting the neighbours, chaddar wrapped around her frail figure. Further off, Aasiya could spot Hassan coming down the dirt path. She had half a mind to throw him in the water, smug face floating downstream.

Hassan's arrival meant her mother and grandmother's attention turned to him. They fussed over the tiny beads of sweat on his forehead, offered him glasses of water, and stroked his hair while he basked in the glory. The two women asked him about his day and worried over him working too hard. Aasiya rushed to get the dishes in place, sweating profusely from the exertion. She could smell the sickly sweet, onion-like stench emanating from her armpits. She would need to take a wash for sure.

After lunch was done, Saima and Aasiya were tasked with cleaning the dishes. Dadi Ji offered to help, but time was working against her. Her age was taking a physical toll on her, and she couldn't exert herself for long amounts of time. She fell asleep on the charpoy in the shade of the jamun trees within minutes. Meanwhile, Ami Jan was sewing a small baby-sized garment by hand. Hassan was being no help as usual.

As soon as the dishes were done, Aasiya, unable to bear the stench any longer, grabbed the bucket from the tiny bathroom and made her way to the river. It no longer had strong currents, or maybe she was just old enough to be able to face them now. She had to go quite a way in to be able to fill the bucket. The coolness of the water felt like a relief. It was like being saved by a cool prince from a fiery hellhole.

Night had settled in by the time Abu came home. He threw a stone in the water, blaming and cursing it for the lack of crop.

The river watched in silence.

"...because, of course, she's our daughter now. We worry for her reputation in the village. Besides wearing a burqa is respectable in our religion," Nasreen Khala managed to squeeze out before resuming her consumption of the *pakoras* and tea.

Ami Jan just nodded, eye bags prominent as ever. Aasiya sat obediently in the corner of the room, empty tea-tray in hand. Outside, she could hear her father and brother chatting with Abdul. He was going on about his newest job in the factory; his fifth in two months. He kept throwing in how it was temporary and how he was destined to be the owner of a massive farm. Abu and Hassan agreed left and right.

After the mother and son left, Aasiya cleared up the dishes. Abu came inside with Hassan, the latter looking a little stony. She could already tell what conversation he was about to bring up and made herself scarce.

"Abu...," Hassan began.

Her father sighed before saying, "*Beta*, I know what you're going to say. We will find you a wife, I promise. But let us fulfil our responsibility with Aasiya first. She's 16, if she doesn't marry now, no one will want her, and she will be stuck in the house. Once she goes, we will find you a girl too, I promise."

Hassan huffed but went quiet. Aasiya knew he was frustrated that Abdul, who was his classmate, would be getting married first. It annoyed her that he was more focused on finding himself a wife rather than wishing for his sister's well-being in another house. In *her* house, as Ami Jan had drilled into her. Aasiya's home was no longer with her parents, but rather with her future husband and mother-in-law.

She stepped outside for some air. It scared her how rapidly everything had happened. She was to be a *wife*. It made her feel a little giggly, though. A lot of her friends had gotten married or were engaged. They would always tell Aasiya she wouldn't understand their conversations, since she was just a kid. Now, she was like them, finally an adult! Her mother would always tell her stories about finding her *Shehzadah* or Prince Charming one day. Now her dreams were a reality.

Lost in her daydreams, she made her way over to the graves by the riverside. Wildflowers grew over the four of them; two adult-sized, two infant-sized. Her two brothers never managed to get a name, dying in childbirth. Her grandmother peacefully lay beside them, next to grandfather. The river gurgled, trickling down the vast plains. Spring was in full bloom.

Aasiya made her way over to the shallow water. The fish were long gone, and the river was a muddy, chemical-infused stream. She could see her own hazy reflection in the rainbow circlets amidst the brown sediments. She stood at the pinnacle of youth; a fresh round face, eyes darkened with *kajal* and a thick black braid. No wonder Abdul had come running for her hand in marriage!

"Aasiya, come inside! Where's your *chaddar*? Be careful, you foolish girl. You're not a child anymore, you can't just step out without covering yourself anymore," Ami Jan yelled, suddenly appearing, dragging her inside roughly, creating ripples in the water.

"There's no one around! It's not a big issue," Aasiya huffed.

"Everyone be damned. You are not to step foot out of the house without a burqa or a *chaddar* at the very least. Did you not hear Nasreen Aapa? You must do as she and Abdul say, you hear me?"

The ripples spread along the water, disturbing its surface as the two women argued.

The water struggled against itself.

Obedience. That was Aasiya's newest lesson for the next several weeks. Spring was coming to an end by the time her marriage date was arranged. It was earlier than expected, but her parents wanted her in her own place before summer.

In the days leading up to it, her mother drilled all kinds of lessons into her. *'Listen to your husband. Never raise your voice. Do the housework, help your mother-in-law. Don't complain. Be the backbone of the family. Never waiver.'*

The young woman honestly didn't believe it was as big a deal as her mother was making it out to be.

When the day of the event came, it was chaos. All kinds of khalas hovered over Aasiya, fretting over this and that. The tiny hut was cramped with women who had come for the ceremony. The overwhelming mixture of scents in the air stung the eyes and made it difficult to breath.

The older women tutted over Aasiya's clothes; each arranged it to her own liking. They tugged at her hair and poked it with hairpins to set it in place. Bright red lipstick was smeared on her. The entire time, the chatter didn't falter. They kept giving her knowing looks.

*'Say goodbye to peace and quiet.'*

*'Life will never be the same again, girlie.'*

*'Best of luck. Childhood is over now.'*

*'Time to become a woman.'*

Aasiya felt as if she were in a daze when the heavy red *dupatta* was finally thrown over her head. Nasreen Auntie patted her head and murmured in approval. Finally, after what felt like forever, the *Maulvi Sahab* was ushered in.

It felt like the world had paused. She suddenly felt scarily alone. All the women stared at her, waiting for her to say those two fateful words. Even her mother felt like a stranger. Instinctively, Aasiya tried to tune her ears to the soothing melody of the river.

She couldn't hear it.

"*Qabool hai.*"

No rush of the water.

"*Qabool hai.*"

No crash of the waves.

"*Qabool hai.*"

Makeup-caked women offered her toothy congratulations. Her mother wiped tears and put on a smile. Food was passed around and inhaled, the main motive of the guests accomplished. Time passed in a whirl. Eventually, a thick chaddar was wrapped around her and she was led outside to where her family stood. Her family: husband and mother-in-law!

Women, who practically raised her in the small neighbourhood, wailed and wiped tears. Her mother was being consoled. Her father put his hand on Aasiya's head and uttered a blessing. Her brother watched over her protectively as she walked towards the rented car that would take her to her new home.

Aasiya turned her head back towards her old life as she walked away from it. She watched as the water looked further and further away.

The car started up.

The flowers on the graves withered, and the river went silent.

"Amma! Amma! Tell him to stop pulling my hair!" Aimal shrieked, swatting at her little brother.

Aasiya sighed. She pulled her youngest son away from her daughter before resuming her task. She added the last stitch to the cloth and held it up to see the final look.

It would have to do. The mistress of the tiny house they lived in paid her a small sum to stitch her clothes. It wasn't much, but situations called for the extra money.

A loud yell from the children told her Abdul was back from work. She heaved herself off the floor and walked towards the door. On her way she passed the window and glanced at the haggard figure looking back at her. With a grimace she continued forward.

"What's for lunch?" Abdul asked, throwing himself onto the rickety charpoy.

"Lentils with bread. We're out of flour, so there's just enough dough to make one *roti* for you." Aasiya stated while rolling her eyes and waiting for the reaction.

"Just one?! What the hell am I supposed to do with one *roti*, woman? I slave all day just to come home and starve?!"

"Maybe if you didn't keep quitting jobs and earned enough money, we wouldn't be in this situation!"

And the same old argument started up again.

It was times like these when Aasiya would miss being a child. She couldn't believe she thought an adult's life was going to be fun and interesting. Stupidity really runs rampant in children. She used to dream of Princes, lush green fields, riches beyond one's imagination and a future as crystal clear as the river water once used to be.

Instead, she was stuck with a lazy husband, screaming children, strained beyond her capabilities and feeling as dried out as the river water now was. Such was life at twenty.

Later the same day, she went to her brother's house. He had officially inherited it from their parents, who lived with him along with his wife. She would go there when she needed to get out of the house, angry and frustrated with her husband. It happened a little too often.

Aasiya arrived balancing little Fawad on her hip, while the other two children were handled with her free hand. As she walked down the path, she thought of how lively the area used to be. Now there were just a few scattered huts and tents left; people forced to move to the main village or city due to poverty. Most of the earning came from agriculture, but the farms were forced to shut down.

Children ran around, some barefoot. Babies wailed out of hunger, while tired mothers shushed them. Elderly men stooped with the weight of bundles of branches, carrying them from the dying forest to their homes.

It was a miserable sight. Everything looked bleak.

Aasiya's children ran into the house, Aimal taking Fawad and leaving Aasiya standing outside the doorstep. She found herself looking out at the shallow trickle of water. Slowly, she made her way over to it.

There was an overflow of graves several meters away from the water's edge. The earth on them was barren despite the onset of spring.

It took a while to find the five original graves. Aasiya went and stood by them, uttering a quick prayer for each. She paused at the fifth.

Saima Bajwa. 11 years old.

Cholera had reduced her sister's body to a frail nothingness. There hadn't been enough money to seek out treatment and thinking of the little girl still pained Aasiya.

She sat on the ground, looking out over all the grave headstones. The land looked like it had been drained of life. Where there was once greenery, was now misery. Maybe water was what had given the earth life, but now it was all gone.

There she sat feeling just as drained as the earth, aging earlier than she should be, feeling the strain of all her inner turmoil.

The water choked and struggled. Aasiya tried to breathe.

What a sad thing to see.

A land without sustenance, a woman without life.

Watch as it trickles away.

Watch; away the water drains.

*From Urdu to English:*

Abu: Father

Ami Jan and Amma: Mother

Burqa: Head to toe veiled covering, usually used by rural Muslim women

Chaddar: Cloth used for covering head and body

Chappal: Slippers

Chotti: Little Girl

Dadi Ji: Grandmother

Dupatta: Scarf or head covering

Karahi: Wok

Kajal: Eyeliner

Khalas: Aunts

Maulvi Sahab: the local mosque's religious lead

Pakoras: Fritters

Puttar and Beta: Child, in Punjabi language

Qabool Hai: Saying 'I Do' while taking the marriage vows

Roti: A type of thin, tortilla-like bread cooked on hot skillet

Shalwar: Trousers

# CHARLOTTE MORAN

# *The Death of the Ticket Collector*

G randad has lived in his train carriage for as long as I can remember. He found it in a scrapyard near Brecon in Wales in 1973. It was a rotted carcass of soft and spongy wood which fell down in crumbs when he walked through the door. Once upon a time it had been a passenger carriage, long and thin with three compartments, an office for the ticket master, a luggage room and a bathroom. There was nothing left of the people who had once used the carriage save for a dusty ticket collector's hat. Grandad walked out of the scrapyard with that hat on, £50 poorer. He stored the carriage in the field of a friend that lay deep in the shadow of the mountains of Bannau Brycheiniog, where the weeds grew over until it was a half-natural beast. I can imagine it now, metal glittering in rays of sunlight, waiting patiently for Grandad to finally come home.

He didn't move in though, not until my grandmother died in 2001. My parents argued with him about it for months. I was only two and a half and they were insistent that he move in with them instead and help them with me, but he had other plans and I honestly don't blame him. The oak of the train had been punctured by wood worms and the roof had caved in, so he stayed in an aluminum caravan for the five years it took to renovate the carriage. I remember racing around that relic of a time long past, with its brown panelling and the constant smell of oxtail soup. All the while the mountains watched us as a tiny speck of a bearded man politely asked a little boy to stand back so he wouldn't get hit by the splinters flying out from the original roof boards. It's a wonder I lived past the age of five.

But even back then, I dreamt of the train. Grandad had painted it green and I had promptly decided that it was Percy from *Thomas the Tank Engine*. Grandad always said that he was a 'cyw', like me — a happy-go-lucky baby bird. I imagined that the train had a face like Percy's and would chat away to it. In my dreams, though, the face was not human but instead that of an owl. Every night, two giant black eyes would stare down at me as I played around the carriage. The two grey halves of the face were cut through the middle by a deep black line running down to the beak. The moon was always full in those dreams but I could only see it in the reflection of those vast, flickering eyes. It didn't bother me as much as it should have, looking back; I was content to play in the weeds beneath this watcher. Sometimes there were lanterns lit in the windows of the train but the door was so clogged up with knotweed and brambles that I could never get in to investigate. Occasionally the owl face would open its beak and I'd hear a voice calling out into the night asking for 'tickets, please'. I never saw the owner of that voice though, not until I was much older.

Grandad finished renovating the carriage when I was seven. My parents made him host a large party, and spent the entire time acting as if they were proud of him for completing the project rather than having fought him every step of the way. I remember him lifting me up to put bunting over the door before all the guests came, and sharing a secret sip of beer with him. That was just like him; he was always mild-mannered and polite, but he had a rebellious streak in him that flared up occasionally. He refused to read books in any language but Welsh, which he explained as a by-product of his school days when he'd be beaten for not speaking English. It became our own secret language that I hid from my parents even to this day.

My cousins were still babies, so I played by myself at that party. I went to look for bugs around the back of the carriage, where the wildflowers had grown high and untamed. However, as I walked out of sight of the party, I saw a man standing in the knee-deep grass. He had a smart looking uniform on, with a sharp navy jacket and a peaked cap that somehow buried his bearded face deep in shadow despite the mid-afternoon sunshine. A polished metal plate on his hat read 'ticket collector' with an engraving of a tawny owl below.

"Hello young man. Ticket, please?" he held out his hand expectantly.

He spoke with a thick Welsh accent like Grandad's.

We stood there in the sunlight for a long time. I couldn't see his eyes but the edge of his lip had curled in a kindly way and I wasn't scared. I just didn't know what to say—I didn't have a ticket to give him—so I said nothing.

After a while, he dropped his hand.

"Until the next time." He tipped his cap and walked around the edge of the carriage and out of sight. I was still standing there, staring after where he'd gone, until my mother came to scold me for not being sociable. I asked Grandad about him when he tucked me into bed that night.

"Sounds like a ghost to me, cyw." He stroked his beard and hummed. "It doesn't sound like he means you any harm but perhaps we should find you a ticket." Rising up from the bed, he left the room and soon returned with a large folder. Plastic folders fluttered as he tipped it open, revealing pages of aged yellow slips of paper. They were the train tickets from every journey he'd ever taken. Together we looked through the pages as he pointed out stations that had been long closed and trips that had led to specific events in his life. I eventually picked out a ticket from Merthyr Tydfil to Brecon from 1953; it seemed only fitting, considering that the carriage had come to rest beneath mountains glimpsed from the windows of that journey. If the ticket collector was looking for a sign of the carriage's final resting place, he would find it with me.

I anxiously awaited the return of the ticket collector, but it would be another four years until I saw him again. By then it seemed a visit on par with seeing a fairy or a mermaid as a child; you truly believed that you had seen one until you looked back years on and realised that it must have been a glimmering dragonfly or an errant seal's tail whipping away into the surf. In other words, I still dreamt of the train but the lights inside had vanished.

Then, when I was ten or eleven years old, I had a new dream. I was in a dance hall with shadowed couples who spun in tight turns through the room, waltzing to music that I couldn't hear. Owls sat on the shadowed beams of the high ceiling. I could see the women's tightly curled hair and the men's arms wrapped around their waists, but there were no faces to be found. I had the sudden thought that, maybe like the conductor, they were not here for me.

The dark wood panelled walls were interspersed with high arched windows. As I made my way over to one, I felt the floor beneath me begin to vibrate, as a deep rumbling purr rolled its way over the room. The previously still landscape outside the windows began to shift away and I felt myself feeling the need to grip the edge of a side table to steady myself. I stared at the blurred outside until a whistle startled me out of my thoughts, and I began to scramble in search of an exit. The swish of the skirts, the squeak of shoes on polished hardwood, the scrape of tree branches along the windows was all too much. I threw myself under a table and sobbed.

When I woke up, the ticket collector was standing outside my window. I never closed those curtains; we were in the middle of nowhere, and none of the popular hiking routes went near us. It was the same spot he had been in all those years before, except now there was a bedroom for me to sleep in, with a window that Grandad had finished installing only last week. It had been salvaged from a different train carriage, so it had a middle partition that could be unlatched and rolled up. After a second, the train conductor politely knocked on the window.

It was so absurd, I laughed. I wasn't scared of this stranger, even though he was nearly definitely a ghost. Rolling out of bed, I hunted through the bedside drawer until I found the ticket I had picked out all those years ago. Then I hoisted up the window. It was a heavy wooden frame that scraped upwards as I let the fresh air in.

"Bore da and good morning to you Sir. May I see your ticket?"

I held out the ticket from Merthyr to Brecon and he inspected it for a second before clipping the corner.

"Very good Sir. I will see you when your journey has finished." He tipped his cap, and as he raised his head I caught a glimpse of something higher into the shadow, a cheekbone and the end of a curl.

"Hang on, when will that be? Excuse me?" I called out to him as he strode away. I jumped down from the window and ran out of my room, right out of the carriage and into the meadow but he had already disappeared.

He was right in the end. The next several years took me down a path that began with the realisation that I was gay, and ended with a dramatic argument that led me to the door of the train carriage one stormy autumn evening. The rain stroked the windows of the carriage as Grandad fussed about in his usual gentle manner, getting me a towel and a cup of tea as I tried in vain to calm myself down. I explained it all to him in between fits of sobbing, not expecting much from him—he was in his mid-eighties at that point, and the older generations didn't exactly have the best reputation for being understanding of that sort of thing—but he listened without judgement. When I finished speaking, he reached over and put his hand on my shoulder.

"You always have a place here, cyw. Whoever you become, as long as you wish. There will always be a home here for you that accepts you as you are, and any man would be lucky to have you as his love."

In that moment, I swear I felt the carriage rumble under our feet. Letting out a purr, it seemed to be shifting and settling in for a long and peaceful nap. Someone walked past the carriage of the window and I felt, rather than saw, the nod of the ticket collector as he passed by on his rounds.

The next few weeks were hard—I'd never seen Grandad as angry as when my parents came to take me home. He sent me outside to collect dandelions for tea, like he had done when I was young and needed distracting, but I could hear the yelling even on the far sides of the field. It led to a truce of sorts: they wouldn't mention my sexuality, and I wouldn't either. I don't think anyone was really surprised when I moved out at eighteen and barely kept in contact.

The last time I saw the ticket conductor was a year after Grandad's funeral. He died in his sleep, in the carriage that he'd revived from its scrapyard grave. We buried him in a cemetery in Brecon and then I just...moved in. I only went to visit for a day, to take some books, but everything was dusty so I started to clean. The smell of the wildflowers drifted through the windows and wrapped around me like vines, tying me there. I couldn't bring myself to leave, and decided instead to stay the night. Three weeks later, I drove back to my flat in Cardiff and packed the rest of my possessions.

I cried most days. I watered his plants. I set up my computer, got an internet connection sorted, started working online. I fed the owls that swooped by in the night. My boyfriend came to visit every weekend, and never asked me to leave, even though he must have spent a fortune on petrol. I even grew a beard like Grandad's. One day I looked in the mirror and saw, not myself, but the twin of the aged photographs on the walls from Grandad's youth.

And every night I entered the train carriage, and my grandad was there. I would run towards him as the carriage rotted around me, wood worms crawling through the floor, blood dripping through the ceiling, hands of passengers reaching out from the compartments. He would disappear into the darkness at the far end of the train in a flutter of wings and I would always be too late.

And yet I stayed.

Time comes and goes and the rumbling never ceases. I am gifted a pin badge with an engraving of a tawny owl by my granddaughter. When night falls, I pin it to my jacket and walk away from life and into the past. There is a boy in a field, looking for bugs amongst the knotweed. I look down at him from under the shadowed brim of my peaked cap, and smile.

"Hello young man. Ticket, please."

*(This story was inspired by Alan Postlethwaite's poem* Poetry in Motion*)*

THALIA PETERSON

# *Pareidolia*

I lower myself onto the bench. Slowly. I'm not the kid I used to be. Children scream as they race each other around the concrete playground, the occasional straggler toppling off his skateboard and falling to the ground in a furiously embarrassed ball of despair. He will eventually come to and be off once again, tormenting the soles of his little Nikes and grating the skin off his red, weeping knees.

Eventually, the chill will nip at sweaty necks and the sky will reach a darkness that will start to fizzle at the edge of one's vision. The street lights will turn on and those with mobiles will receive passive-aggressive texts from their parents, which will either result in a heated argument at home or some risky white lies that definitely won't become problematic later.

For now, the sun is still a healthy slither over the rooftops in the distance, and I find myself drifting lazily off into thought as the motion around me continues to stir up the skeletons of leaves and discarded ice cream wrappers.

It reaches my attention that a little boy is watching me.

I had been surveying the scene with an uninterested eye, considering my history with the skate park and comparing my lost skills to that of some foreign teenager, only to reach the unblinking gaze of the child.

He's partially hidden by the constant whirlwind of moving bodies, but through the flashes of gangly high school dropouts and fleshy kids with mullets, I manage to spy his pale face.

"Roger!" he shouts. As if worried that I hadn't heard him, he repeats this a couple of times and beckons me with a chubby hand.

I gesture to my chest, confused, and also disturbed. He seems confident that he knows me, and upon his continuous invitations to join him in the midst of the terrifying commotion of second-hand scooters, I find myself carefully picking my way over to where he waits.

We have to stand relatively close together, otherwise we pose as an irritating obstacle to those who actually want to get around. I compare our heights; me, towering threateningly above a six, maybe seven-year-old boy, who looks naive and innocent in comparison. I massage my temples but look down at him as patiently as I can.

"Roger," he says with a strangely mature smile, "it *is* good to see you."

"How do you know my name?" I ask, narrowing my eyes a fraction and studying him cautiously.

The youth motions to my chest and I peer down, tugging my shirt out a little so that I can catch a glimpse of the dull name badge.

"I see," is all I tell him.

"What did you do today, Roger?" The little boy questions me with an air of childish curiosity but verging on confidence—as if he already knows the answer that he will receive. However, when I reply, he looks believably interested.

"I was at a funeral," I say. "As the director. Do you, er, know what that means?"

"Of course! Somebody died!" he shouts, and I have to pat his shoulder and hiss between my teeth a bit to get him to quiet down.

"Look, are you lost? Did you come here alone?"

"I'm always here, Roger!"

"Yes, but where are your parents?"

His little face breaks into a grin.

The intense throb of a migraine hits my temples and I stumble to the left a little bit.

My acquaintance quickly directs me back to my original placement before someone on a skateboard can bowl me over.

"Careful," he instructs, "it's very easy to fall in this place."

"Well, thanks," I grunt, one hand pressed to the side of my face while the other is resting on a nearby ramp. "I'm afraid that I should be going. It's..." I check my wristwatch and tap the glass for added emphasis, as the child looks thoroughly confused by my sudden attempt at departure, "...quite late, and I'm quite cold. Perhaps you should head home to your folks too, no? Get some food in you."

I manage two paces before I'm hit with another wave of nausea and the dull, impending beat of tension. I feel sticky hands gripping my own and settling me comfortingly onto a bench that smells of offensive energy drinks and long abandoned socks.

I groan and cradle my head in my hands, frustrated with the ill-timing of this incessant aching. I feel the spidery breath of the kid next to me and his needy fingers picking at a loose thread in the waistband of my dress pants.

I crack open an eye and turn to look at him again.

"Can you tell me something?" he asks me softly, barely audible against the sound of seagulls alighting onto the street lights and kids taking the long walk back from school. His voice is neatly-trimmed and well-practised, as if he's had this same conversation with himself every night.

I nod, but even that hurts the flesh, the blood, the very bones under my skin. "Do you remember me, Roger?" With this he tilts his head a little closer, a little better in the light, for me to scrutinize the alien features and memories stretched across his eyes.

After a moment, I lean back, and massage my forehead. "I'm sorry, but I really don't..."

"Do you remember what they said about you?" he continues, cocking that pale face of his like a bird.

"Said what?"

"Why are you even here, Roger?"

I shrug, distressed that I feel at fault in this situation somehow. "I... like it here. I came here when I was your age, and younger."

The continuous blur of sweating bodies circling around the skate park like a swarm of flies is impacting the suffering of my skull. The motion isn't quite smooth—it's more like watching a form of movement under a quickly flickering lounge light. The blacks, the browns, the reds and the blues squish and contort into a foul rainbow of teenage trends and corrupted society.

"You had a lot of friends, didn't you, Roger? You always told me I was special, but I never believed you. Do you remember who you went with to play here forty-one years ago? Two boys. You should guess their names."

Every syllable sends a shrill pain into my head and I groan. "I don't..."

"Roger, you goose!" The kid chuckles. "It was me! You took me and Harrington. The tall one. Do you remember now?"

I whip my head around. "Clyde Harrington? I don't know who you've been talking to or what this is about, but seriously, kid, how do you know me?"

An idea hits him. He jumps up, rejuvenated, and takes one of my hands again. I hobble after him through the midst of the feral mob of rollerbladers and young adults. He takes us to the damaged concrete staircase and up to the imposing, almost vertical ramp that I never mastered as a schoolboy.

"So what?" I hiss, cupping my head. However, I can't help but feel a worm of something slithering through my mind.

"You thought it would funny," he tells me. "You took us to the edge and made us watch. Harrington thought it was funny, but I wanted to go home."

"Made you watch...what?"

"You had your father's skateboard," he says. With a pale finger, he points generally to below us, where a couple of confused children have their eyes set on me as they chew gum, and a starling is eating the few remaining crumbs of a pizza. "You barely knew how to ride it."

I remember now.

I remember the walk from school, blithely chatting and planning the afternoon. I remember not being alone. I remember lashing out every now and then, even at my tender age, at somebody I did not willingly bring along. He came along anyway.

"You said I should try, because I was being a baby. You made me stand here, at the edge, and I kept telling you, over and over, that I didn't want to." The boy's lips twitch, a smile barely curbed.

Breathing becomes a task and I do so heavily. Back then, I could smell the sweat that glistened on our foreheads. I could hear Harrington behind me, egging me on.

"You grew tired of my tears. You didn't want me to whine, or cry like a girl, or tell a grown-up. I made you so angry, so bitter that you barely had a moment to think."

My companion no longer has the voice of a child. He sounds like me.

"You turned around. You looked me in the eye." A pause. "You know what happens next."

I remember the way my fist connected with his arm. It was meant to *hurt* him. He stumbled, clumsy, delicate feet tilting in all the wrong ways and losing balance.

I had expected everything to stop. All around, I expected the deafening, constant crawl of the crowd, the countless gossamer legs glittering and shivering mechanically across the vast, slick surface of a concrete arthropod, to *finally* stop. I *craved* that silence.

Instead, it took a few moments for any one person to register the still body on the ground, or the sound of the aftermath of its descent.

I sway, I step backwards, and I cradle my stomach as if the extra barrier of my fingers will keep the semi-digested food inside. These fresh memories plague me like a sickness under the skin, and I turn to the little boy I killed in anguish.

But he has merrily skipped back down the steps and into the crowd, where the colours once again lose any individual meaning and become all but nothing to an offended viewer.

I feel my weight quickly lowering downwards and I sense the grating of little rocks under my fingertips. My legs dangle over the ramp and the rubber soles of expensive shoes stare down at an ancient crime scene.

"It isn't your fault," I can hear my mother whispering, "You didn't do anything wrong...there's no need to say sorry to me, darling. He must have gone there alone and tripped. There's really just nothing you could have done. Harrington has already told me that you two spent the afternoon at Jimmy's."

Perhaps if we had, my brother would still be alive.

## KANTAPHAT PINAREE

# *Elegy for a Machine*

S orry to interrupt, but...what are you doing?"
    It was March, when winter turned to spring, and the wind brought with it the scent of tulips and daffodils.

"Mourning."

The air was crisp and cool, reminiscence of the first sip of a chilled drink on a hot summer day. Overhead, a kite flew, gliding across the cloudless sky like a brushstroke across a brilliant blue canvas.

"Mourning?"

Around us was naught but grass as far as the eye could see. Grass, blemished only by a long, winding railway track, almost like a black scar over a sea of green.

"Yes."

The old man had on a buttoned-up, red and black checkered T-shirt and a pair of well-worn blue overalls, riddled all over with burn marks and fabric patches of various colours. A white, bushy beard adorned his wrinkled face, complementing his blue eyes, the same blue as the sky.

Atop his head of white hair was a plain black cap with the word 'Conductor' embroidered in white. In his hand was a violin, its mahogany frame gleaming majestically under the morning sun.

"What are you mourning?"

Wordlessly, he pointed to where the railway track disappeared over the edge. There, billowing smoke out of its chimney, was an old steam locomotive, slowly making its way towards us.

"...an old friend."

This particular train was nothing special. The locomotive itself

Kantaphat Pinaree

was an old, outdated model from the early days of rail transport, outpaced long ago by more modern designs. Its exterior, painted in the classic red and black, showed significant wear, with the majority, if not all, of its parts having been replaced at some point in its lifespan.

On its side, embroidered in gold, was its name: *The Wolfsstatt Limited*.

"A train?"

The old man smiled sadly.

"Yes," he paused, "an old friend."

I looked at him quizzically.

"An old friend?" I echoed in disbelief, "But it's just a train."

He turned to me.

His gaze, with those kind, blue eyes, held mine.

"She faithfully travelled along her route for over sixty years. She was a courier who brought letters from distant friends. A traveller who took people where they needed to go. Who still shoulders a duty that no one else would. She is, to me, an old friend."

I stared at him.

"But it's just a machine."

His smile grew sadder.

"Can a machine not have a soul?"

"Well..."

"Can a machine, who I have known since I was sixteen, a machine who was there when I met my first friends, a machine who was there when we were sent to the front and waiting for us when we returned, who was there the day I married the love of my life and there the day I buried her. A machine who was there for all the good and the bad, who was there for both my brightest and darkest of days...can she not have a soul?"

I opened my mouth, but no words came out.

He looked back at the train.

"She is an old friend. The only one I could ever ask for."

"I...I'm sorry about what I said."

He shook his head.

"It's alright," he said, "you didn't know."

I shaded my eyes from the sun and looked towards the train, its metal body glinting against the sun.

52

"Why are you mourning, exactly?"

He gazed at the locomotive, still perhaps several minutes away from us.

"She's being decommissioned. Replaced by a newer model. This is her last trip."

"...I see," I replied empathetically. "I'm sorry."

Once again, he shook his head.

"Don't be. It's...it's for the best."

"For the...best?"

"Mm."

"Look," he gestured around us at the endless grassland, "what do you see?"

"Well," I scratched my head, "just us, the tracks, the grass..."

"Exactly," he smiled at me, tears brimming in his eyes, "there should have been more. There should have been twenty people. Thirty. Everyone who worked with her and counted her as a friend. Old Renard the Engineer, Frau Blauch, Julian from the ticket office... we should have all been here to send her off."

I imagined all those people standing around him: another old man in a wheelchair waving the locomotive off with a smile, an old lady weeping into a handkerchief, a younger man comforting her...

"If only I had the courage to ask them to let her rest sooner. Last year, we would have had five. The year before, eleven. But it's too late for regret. Too late."

He wiped away the tears and bowed his head.

"At least I am here. Another year and perhaps...perhaps there would be no one left. No one...yes, I'm glad they're doing it now, so at least one of us can see her off."

A few more minutes passed, and the locomotive inched ever closer.

"Do you know what she does?" the old man broke the silence.

"She's a daily service from *Wolfsstatt* to *Vilstein*, right?"

"Aye, been running since 1892." He gazed fondly into the distance. "But, really, she's much more than that."

He pointed east, along the track.

"Each morning she would pick up mail from *Wolfsstatt*. There would be a cheque from the watchmaker Graham Tanner to his brother and bedridden mother, a package from Doctor Schmidt to five different patients, a container of coal bound for Herr Graf's factory, and a bundle of letters for various different residents of *Vilstein*. On Saturdays, Graham himself would board the train along with Sarah Reller, who was visiting her sweetheart; Doctor Schmidt, who needed to do a weekly checkup on his patients; and Hans Hauser, who just liked to sit and watch the world rush past him through his cabin window."

He turned and pointed west, down the opposite end of the track.

"She would get to *Vilstein* by noon, where she would then pick up a shipment of whiskey for *The Alte Kneipe*, another shipment of iron outbound from Herr Graf's factory, a letter from little Martin Weber for his father, which Frau Blauch the stationmaster always personally pays for, and a letter from Maria Kuper to her pen pal four towns over."

His expression was nostalgic as he gazed back at the locomotive.

"She would then make it back to *Wolfstatt* by evening and rest up for the next day. She was the bridge connecting the two towns. She connected friends and family. She brought people together and took people where they needed to go. She was the lifeblood of both towns."

I looked at the train again, with its axles cycling in a simple, circular motion, slowly moving the wheels forward along the tracks.

"It's a surprise that such a simple set of motions could achieve so much."

"Aye. Every big thing is always made up of little things. A mountain is as much a mountain as the small, individual rocks that it's made up of. A wheel can only move so quickly from the initial motion imparted upon it."

The old man swept his hands across the grassland, and I saw what he meant.

The swaying of each individual blade of grass and how they came together to make a gentle wave across the plains. The beautiful blue of the sky and how it wasn't one blue but a coalescence of cerulean, cobalt, sapphire, azure, and so, so much more, coming together to make that blue unmatched by any one of its components. The green grass and the blue sky, how they were better together than either alone.

"Just like the ol' girl," the old man nodded, "she's made up of only metal and smoke...but to everyone here, she is so much more than the sum of her parts."

The sun was still high in the sky, and the landscape still the same as it always was when the train approached the spot where we were standing.

I turned to the old man for the last time.

"It's time, then?"

He did not reply, for he was no longer there.

"Old man?" I looked around.

There was no one here but me.

I adjusted my cap and, looking down, found the violin in my hand.

Then the weight of the years fell on me.

My arms wearied and my back ached. I felt the wrinkles on my face and the beard on my chin. I felt the heat of the sun and the bitter cold of the wind.

And I laughed.

Of course, why would anyone else be here, out on the tracks?

Why would there be a clear sky and endless grassland?

Why would a train have taken so long to cross this small strip of land?

No.

The sky was cloudy and dull.

Surrounding me was a dense deciduous forest with a small line cutting through it to allow for the railway tracks.

There were no tulips or daffodils, just the heavy smell of smoke.

And, next to the tracks, stood only me.

"Alone, alone, just me left to mourn," I sighed. "An old man with half a mind who poured his thoughts to the wind."

I watched *The Wolfsstatt Limited*, which had just come into view perhaps only a minute ago and will reach me at any moment.

And, without another word, I hefted up the violin and brought the bow onto the strings.

To play an elegy for a machine.

CATHERINE SAUNDERS

# *Figurehead*

The day before we reached the distant promised land, my mother died.

Mother, who folded the washing with morning sunlight dappled across her face. Mother, who cooked all childhood lunches in sanguine silence, stifled by the spitting of the hob and the chirping of crickets in the undergrowth. Mother, who used to play her cello in the evening, permeating the air with a gentle song like the flap of bird wing into the night.

Sometimes, I catch myself humming the final notes. The slow, bowing descent into silence. The moment after the song's cessation... it would fester. Low vestiges of the cello's mournful cry would linger in the midsummer humidity, clasping onto their last breaths. Simmering. You could feel the vibrations beneath your skin. I used to try and hold them, like clutching at a half-forgotten dream in the morning. For a precious moment longer, I could feel that last note. Then, it would gasp and dissipate. The long drone of bees usurped my mother's cello and we'd lapse into silence.

I look back fondly now. Standing beside a pond, pushing paper boats into the water and watching the ripples glide endlessly in their wake; we'd race them, locking our tiny sailors in competition. Catching bugs in glass jars and listening to her ramble about the banded centipede while I peered inside at the writhing creature. Those long summer days spent on the terrace, staring up at the stars and not yet wondering their names, nor searching among their ranks for those who are lost. When I had not yet grown my armour.

Then the motion began, and since then I have not known a

moment's peace.

"Naya? Naya, come here." The words bungled together, spoken through a mouthful of cotton. A vague shape of my sister materialised from the darkness, entering the halo of dim lamplight. The subterranean glow draped across her. Her raggedy bunny drooped from her fist, held by one ear. Then, her hands were still chubby when they balled up, and her eyes were still big and wondering and full of sleep. Childhood breathed raspingly through her, on its last legs.

I clasped her tiny hand in my own and brushed off her coat; the hem sagged down to her knees while the sleeves hung past her fingertips. One of mine I had shed some years before.

Already I could see the onslaught of worry advancing into her face. Her lips drooped at the corners; her eyebrows were low as she looked up at me smoulderingly. "Where we going? Are we moving houses again?" I wanted to reach up and smooth out the wrinkles that folded across her fresh face, tell her everything was fine. Instead, I turned away. Something that had laid dormant below her skin had started to rouse, and I was terrified of it.

While I stuffed old albums and tins of soup into a bag, she scuttled across the floor, still discovering the extent of her own mobility. Something about her top-heavy tumbling reminded me of a newborn faun on unsteady legs; it hasn't found its balance. It hasn't found its limitations.

Three men paced around me while I packed, stepping over me as if I wasn't there. They insidiously drained our living room of all its furniture. I watched them as they heaved out the sofa, the armchair, the cabinets—they even sliced through the curtains, lacerating them with curved daggers. And again, they fled the room, arms heavy with the fabric of my youth.

Gradually, my home emptied around me like an exsanguination. Each removal was a stab to the heart. All relics and familiarities of my childhood were crammed into a van on the street below, all pieces of me.

"She must have sold everything to them," Naya said some time later. "We wouldn't be needing it any longer anyway." But she didn't remember them like I did. She'd never seen our mother wrap herself in the curtains while singing a Kurdish song I couldn't understand. She couldn't recall sitting on our mother's lap on the couch, bouncing on her knees and babbling away as babies do.

My mother glided into the room. "Safiya," she said, "have you packed everything?" I wish I could recall the sound of her voice as it washed across the thick silence of the room, laden with terror and tension. She stared at the backpack of all our possessions slumped at my feet. The quiet bloomed around us. All of a sudden, the bag seemed to hunch in on itself, looking more pitiful by the second. Standing in the centre of the empty room, I gazed at the unfamiliar house around me. Then I looked at my mother, because I had no one else left.

She simply smiled. It didn't reach her eyes. "Good girl," she said, picking up Naya effortlessly. "Take that bag, Cherub. The man is waiting in the Square and he'll leave without us if we're not there in half an hour."

The man in the Square was built like an oak, broad-shouldered and imposing. His physique gave the impression he had been beaten by a meat tenderiser and it had stretched out all of his proportions; his biceps alone must have been the width of a girder. A sinuous purple scar stretched between his collarbone and jaw—when we got into his van, he told us a madman with a hatchet had attacked him in Istanbul sometime in the late '90s. My mother must have seen the flickering flame of panic in my eyes, because she leant back and whispered that it had probably been a construction site accident.

"Lucky miss with a steel beam."

As we drove through smoking cities and manoeuvred around chunks of debris, the man picked up other waifs along the way. All were lugging similarly diminutive packs and looked similarly haunted. The whole country carried with it an air of exhaustion; it laced the oxygen there like smoke.

It was a long time before we reached the Aegean Sea. The man-tree deposited us somewhere past the border and sped away with the little money my mother had collected for the furniture. By now, Naya was clamouring for attention and food; of both, we had so little to spare.

My mother tilted her head towards the sun. Her delicate features basked in it, gilded by the midday light. When she opened her eyes, the tarnished brown of her irises melted to toffee.

"We walk from here, girls."

We did. For days. We trekked until our feet were blistered and our legs bitterly sunburnt. Illusions of the ocean danced on the edge of the horizon, always a mile away. Through cities and suburbs and planes of desolation and dust we trudged, following the battered road signs.

Mother sang songs for morale. Each step elicited a syllable from her, as we plodded out her beat.

Every day, the sun beat down at full force. Each night the winds would howl with a vengeance. After a week, I began to think we'd walk until we reached the end of the Earth and had to turn around and return to the empty house we'd left.

But slowly, achingly, we made progress. And finally, real water reared up from beyond the horizon.

When we finally made it to salvation, our victory was short-lived.

The boat was little more than a dinghy with a motor. I doubted it would survive a gale. A whisper of doubt crept into my mind and took root there, plaguing the ounce of hope I allowed myself. But we were piled in nonetheless, layer after layer of human, flesh upon flesh. There must have been fifteen souls crammed into the raft. We huddled in, shoulder to shoulder. It was a wonder it could float; it strained against our weight, yearning to submit to the sea, now speckled with stars like salt spilled across a tablecloth.

For a while, we glided across the surface with little effort. Our destination loomed closer and closer; progress felt inevitable, our hope palpable.

But the next night, a storm brewed from the north.

Rain pelted against the ocean, emotionless. At first, the shower seemed as though it might wane within the hour. The spit of rainfall ebbed and flowed. When the wind began to swirl around us, encasing us in a maelstrom of turbulent water, all promise was dashed against the rocks.

The boat started to undulate. Rearing. Bucking. Crashing back down. One of the boys vomited over the side of the ship.

Silence pooled across the boat.

The motion surged. Up and down and up again. Our boat smashed over the waves. A creeping sensation settled along my back as I peered over the side and sickness swelled in my belly. My reflection distorted in the frothing water and I could discern nothing of the depths.

A shadow passed beneath us.

The boat lurched as if a hunk of metal had slammed against its underbelly. Naya's hand dislodged itself from mine. My heart surged up to my throat. Her tiny body jolted. Mother—

Last night, I opened my eyes and saw her again.

Somehow, she was *ethereal*. When she died, I had not yet learnt that word. By the time I discovered it, it was too late and the time to use it had long since passed me by.

But there she was, ethereal as the moment she left me. What I could make out the most was her mouth, which smiled in its silly sanguine way, and her hands. Calluses rasped across the left and an angry weal arched along her right palm where she had burnt herself while cooking. It curved along her lifeline and disappeared behind her thumb, stretching like a track through mountains.

As I stared at her through simmering waves of heat that distorted her features, her brow furrowed. Her expression shifted almost imperceptibly to a mien of infinite regret and her lips drooped at the sides.

For a moment, the boat was in a glass bottle. Placid sea and empty sky merged into one. There we existed, unarmoured, in a dome of endless blue. Squinting up at the Sun, the sole blemish on the face of the limpid sky, it could have been the eye of a mariner peeking down at his boat in a bottle. My mother must have been the figurehead, alluring and fragile and desperate.

I reached towards her. A baby clutching its hand for its blanket, its fingers outstretched like a starfish.

Then, like dreams tend to do, she flickered. "Mummy," I said. It had been years since I'd said that word and it choked out of my throat on a sob. As I spoke, she dissipated, foundering on the rocks of consciousness.

—Mother stood up. The boat shuddered. On its last legs. The hurricane whipped my hair into my face as I grasped blindly for my mother.

"Mummy!" I screamed. My voice evaporated into the wind. "Mummy!" I had lost sight of Naya. My hair was filling my eyes. Something was coming. I could feel rumbling far below.

Not far below. *Just below.*

Just below, the creaking of the ancient bones of an awakening beast. The shadow beneath us burgeoned impossibly. And only then could I see. Just at the perfect moment, I opened my eyes to see the impossible. The unbearable.

A bleached tendril burst from the water to drag her in.

She faded into the tumult like a paper doll.

And she was gone.

Sometimes I look back upon the unravelling string of my childhood and catch a hint of the notes my mother used to play on blistering evenings.

I have heard her song just once here. One Saturday, in a tube station I cannot name. A woman stood in the corner, back against the Underground tiles and facing the slurry of rush hour commuters. It was a violin—that's what my mother would have said. The woman, draped in a silk scarf and huddling behind a winter coat, played a violin. A cellist is far more difficult a beast to find and tame.

But it took me back home. Each vibrating note, lingering too long, longing to be heard beyond their cessation. If I closed my eyes and held my breath, I could hear the bees buzzing in the treeline beyond our garden. All I had to do was ask its name.

Then my train heaved into the station, and my question was lost forever. But the melody of my mother is undying. It lives beyond its years, and exists without its name.

I believe there is a place, across the sea, where a mother's song is gently fading away. Her children are clamouring for more, laughing over the resonating notes. There, the air is clear and the skies are vast; when they look up into never-ending twilight, they'll see one more star. They won't wonder its name.

In that distant land, alive with swelling song, the air is filled with ghosts.

TESSA SHUTTER

---

## *When a Car Dies on a Deserted Road Does it Make a Sound?*

The car is dying. It's been making the snarling moan of a sick thing for months, but it only started this weak rattle a moment ago. Maybe I couldn't hear the rattle because I was numb. But either way the car's dying. The car windows show nothing but fields, barren by winter's bite. I used to love that Joe lives in the middle of nowhere but now it boils my blood. I want to tear the entire picturesque landscape to shreds and leave the remains hung up on Joe's irritatingly quaint farmhouse door. If I break down and get stranded in this netherworld I'll have Joe's head; well actually, if I ever get that close to that gorgeous head again, I might kiss it and that would be a bad idea for every party involved, so I need to get as far away as possible.

I press on the acceleration and the car hesitantly lurches forward in my bidding; the change of pace is only punctuated by an increase in the volume of the car's weeping. My mind tells me it's ready. The adrenaline that has been pumping through my head like an ocean making everything quieter has worn off. I'm out of the weird hormones that got me out of Joe's house and safely into my car. Now I can feel the tears muscling their way through my eyes and my mind is ready to think about it. The table has been sanitised, all the tools sharpened, and Dr Self-Loathing is prepped to dissect. The conversation being brought into theatre today, the one that's putrid entrails are about to be splayed out on the table is the breakup conversation. Time of death about ten minutes ago. Joe had taken my hand, his skin rugged but his grip gentle, like he was cradling a baby; Joe is the only person who has ever made me feel precious. I let myself cry because I'm in the middle of extra-rural Hampshire and nobody can see me apart from the car and the crows. I don't care about the crows and the car has seen worse.

"Eli," Joe had given it all away the first time he said my name; he was carrying it in his mouth like a bomb, and as he sat me down his fingers danced over my hands like they were barbed wire. I hadn't bothered to answer. The doctor finds this and sends it away for testing. If I'd said something, if I'd changed the subject, if I'd told him I loved him one last time maybe it wouldn't be like this. If I had apologised for... everything, maybe It wouldn't have happened. I had looked up at him, giving him my full attention, gazing into his sombre eyes.

"I think you're a truly incredible person," he said.

I nodded, "Thanks,"

"But I can't do this anymore."

About then was when my brain went into freefall. My consciousness had clawed the air madly, attempting to stop but you can't stop falling until you land.

"Why?"

The doctor also finds an issue with my tone here, I was too harsh, too wounded. Joe did that thing he does when he opens his mouth as if to speak but just mouths for a while like a fish gasping for air; he does it when he can't quite work out what to say.

"Because..." The pauses are also a trademark of Joe carefully curating his sentences, "I love spending time with you Eli, I've been so grateful to have you this past year but I can't trust you,"

I'd been silent for a moment in confusion, the fall speeding up and feeling like the velocity was stealing my voice and my sense "I've never been unfaithful," I had mumbled.

"That's not what I mean," Joe had quickly corrected me with a sweep of his arm, so dramatic it made me jump. "Eli you're loyal, I know that, but I can't trust you not to disappear, I can't trust you not to end up dying in an alley anytime you're not with me."

The doctor agrees with me that that was a cruel move from Joe. "That's not fair, I'm sober now and we have a system, I always call."

"You didn't last month,"

"That was last month,"

"It could be next month given your track record."

I didn't want to keep going back and forth with him, so I fell silent. The doctor says I should have fought harder.

"Eli, I need to dedicate more time to my work, and you know my mum's health isn't going well, I have to be present for her, and…"

I don't remember the other excuses he prattled off, I went back to falling, I went back to trying desperately to find a way to stop.

"I can't spend all my time worrying about you anymore Eli, you need to get help, and I can't give that to you."

My mouth had begun running, smashing through every bit of ammunition I had to make him stay, to make him stop. I begged until I was a desperate wreck and then I begged just a little more until I knew there was no hope, until I could admit defeat. Joe was done. Joe had thrown me away with all his charming compassion and soft touch; he'd managed to do it in such a nurturing, mollycoddling way that I almost didn't realise I was the trash he had picked up and was now being chucked out because I couldn't be fixed.

The doctor has observed all these things, Dr. Self-Loathing has deduced that I put up a bad fight, that I'm useless and that Joe isn't to blame at all, I mean of course Joe isn't to blame. Dr Self-Loathing has finished his autopsy. Cause of death, me.

The car continues, barely. It fights its way up a gentle hill, chugging and sputtering like it might have something to say but I've never been able to communicate with the car before. I wonder if it's trying to talk to me, to get out its last words.

"Don't die on me," I whisper in the gathering darkness, "You're all I have left."

The headlights are dim and the road ahead is only illuminated for a few feet in a faded yellow. I can still see the fields in the low dusk light. In a few hours, when I get home, I'm going to have to tell somebody about this, some of my mutual friends probably already know, Joe may have a told a few, but when I get home I'll tell my mum, or my brother, or whoever is at the door to let me in because I forgot my keys as usual and it will all be real. But for now, as I make my way out of Joe's particular realm of rich, white boy, nobody knows, for now it hasn't really happened yet, it doesn't count. Everyone else is going about their lives thinking it's still Eli and Joe. I miss being a collective, I miss being Joe's. I've had many titles, Joe's boyfriend, Joe's situationship, Joe's hookup, Joe's friend… I never cared really, as long as there was a Joe's in front of it and it didn't end in Ex; my heart is already yearning for the return of that prefix. Neon studs my vision as the snapped windscreen wipers part to show a glowing petrol station, the shell sign like a beacon, a buttery layer of protection in the encroaching night. Technically the car does not need petrol, but I think it would appreciate anything at this point, including a break.

The car struggles into a parking space and I wrestle with the door until it finally gives, and I can clamber out into fresh air. I know it's supposed to be cold; the frost climbing my car bonnet like lace on a wedding dress tells me that, but my body is yet to feel it. I don't think my nervous system has space for the cold right now, it's busy with a knotted tangle of grief, sadness, howling rage and embarrassment. I fill up the car. The petrol gurgles into it and I hope it's going to work some magic because I refuse to be stranded out here, even though I know Joe would probably pick me up because he loves to be a hero. I can't complain; it's not like I didn't love being his charity case.

The man behind the desk in the petrol station smiles at me. Tea steams at his side and I wonder how long he has left on this shift.

"That green one yours?" he asks. The car park is empty; it could only be mine, but I nod as if it wasn't a stupid question.

"It's seen better days," I admit as I watch his eyes scan from the scuffed corners to the mosaic of a rear-view mirror. The man's face creases into a smile, and he runs up the cost on his machine. I don't know how the contraption works.

"Anything else for you?" he offers; his tender question feels like the prod you give a corpse to check if it's alive.

"Vodka." I point at the vodka behind the counter. The man nods. He doesn't ask me for ID which is a rare occurrence; I guess my misery is indicative of adulthood.

"Are you alright, mate?" he asks. "You look like you've seen better days too."

I almost laugh: the car and I have always had a lot in common.

"I'm alright," I say. "Just got dumped, that's all."

The man adds the vodka to the cost, his smile contorting into sympathy.

"That's rough," he says, "You're going to be OK, like you're not going to touch this till you stop driving right?"

I nod.

"Promise me."

I narrow my eyes, does he see the hunger in my gaze, the weak way my body tenses as he threatens to withhold it from me.

"I promise." My tongue wrestles the words out of my mouth.

The man seems satisfied and turns the card reader to me. I tap my card knowing it is now probably empty of funds. There's the usual affirming beep and I hold my hand out for the bottle. It is cool and smooth and everything perfect and the man watches my smile in fear. I go back to my car.

There's barely a difference in the way the car moves but the groaning is quieter. I don't know if that means it's closer or further from death. I think about Joe as I usually do, I think about whether or not he loved me; he must have, he wouldn't have put up with everything if he didn't love me. I can't not think about how Joe has a scar on his lip which I gave him one night when I had gnawed instead of kissed. It was a night when tequila had taken my senses and kindness looked like an attack. I had tried to blame the world for that scar, for making all the attacks violent enough to warrant the defences. But we all knew it was me. Joe also has a scar on his wrist which he obtained from a bathroom sink in some club or other fighting my head to prevent it from drowning in its own vomit. I've managed to put three scars on him in one year. The third traces his collarbone and I have no idea how it happened. The first time I saw it was when I woke up in a hospital bed and saw Joe sitting there, the scab making a dotted road to nowhere above his shirt collar. I remember we spoke at the same time,

"What happened?"

"You're OK." He had ignored my question. "That doesn't matter, all that's important is that you're alive." I also can't stop thinking about how surprised he had been that I'd lived.

I want to talk to Joe. The panging urge to call him and discuss anything he so pleases begins to hit as the car trundles itself onto the motorway, refusing to speed up. The sky is vast and empty, and I can't find the moon. Joe and I used to call most nights, we used to FaceTime over dinner or on errands just so any moment of alone time wasn't wasted, so we could be together even if it was over the artificial magic of Wi-Fi.

My phone sits in the passenger seat and my hands burn to pick it up, to text him, I don't know what I would ever plan to say, I don't really hope to change his mind, Joe always means what he says. I think I just want him not to forget me; that's what I would mean with every text or call or letter, another reminder that I endure, that he hasn't cast me into nothingness. All the missives mean are *I'm still here.*

I have moved a total of forty miles away from Joe. Forty miles of moving on, I ignore the fact my heart and head haven't left his kitchen table. My body is here even though my soul still curls its hands around Joe's and begs him to love it again. When I get home, I can try to forget, I can go to sleep and take a bath and watch three days' worth of television. At home I'm allowed to be heart broken. But I'm on the motorway and I can't stop and start crying because there's a minimum speed limit and three lanes of impatient cars and floodlights and road signs and various LEDs all blinking at me to carry on, blinding me with their cajolement. They don't have time for breakdowns on motorways. Traffic will jam, eyes will be rolled, barricades put up and signs changed; you can't breakdown on motorways. I wish Joe had come to my house to dump me, then he could have left, and I could have lain down and cried into my own sheets, not a dying car. The soon to be automobile corpse is creaking and juddering as gears shift and stick. It's almost driving itself, compromising with me, its broken parts putting a stop to many a request of mine.

I've found the moon. It's hanging low to my right, dyed into a yellow hue; it's crossed with black clouds and almost looks like it's frowning. I shiver under the notion that the moon is judging me, its celestial eyes burning through the car window to assess this particular night traveller, to rake its gaze over tear-stained cheeks and anxiety mussed hair. The moon has taken one look at my rumpled T-shirt and haunted, sunken eyes and knows I am worthless. The moon agrees with Joe's decision.

I haven't forgotten about the vodka. I also haven't forgotten about my promise. Joe has emptied all the fuel out of me, he's hollowed out the feelings and love and thoughts. I feel like I must fill the void of myself with something. When it comes to my personal emptiness, vodka takes up a lot of space.

Trees and sparse fields border the motorway; every so often there is a pretty house worth very little due to this sort of positioning. Being near a road has never bothered me in theory. I like the idea of being on the doorstep of life, a constant soundtrack of migration. Some horses are standing in the field ahead. They're standing very close, and their tails are whisking in the wind. Headlights flash over their eyes but they don't seem to blink; they've seen this all before.

I swing off the motorway, rolling back into country lanes, but now I'm closer, now I'm almost home.

Yesterday Joe had an argument with his mum about the collective noun for a group of hedgehogs. She had been adamant it was a rustle but Joe was certain the term was prickle. While they bickered, proffering forth differing pieces of anecdotal evidence I discreetly googled the answer. Joe had been right. I'd proudly shown everyone the Wikipedia bible of evidence and everybody had conceded. My job was to prove Joe right. That's what a partner's meant to do, isn't it? They're supposed to back their lover up, whatever the case; Joe was always right, or I always made him right. I'm twenty minutes from home. Twenty minutes away from where I can break down in peace, like a car in a garage. At home there are people who can put me back together again. The car dies. I open the bottle and drink as a drowning man gulps air. I'm good at my job.

---

# *The Matchmaker*

Nicholas has finally found a girl stupid enough to date him. Perhaps that's a bit harsh. After 400 years together, I ought to be more sensitive in light of our long relationship.

Still, I can't deny my first reaction was along the lines of 'batten all the windows and plant me on my chimney: a girl whose wit has fled her enough to date that dratted wizard'.

Nick has been trying for a girlfriend for the past century at least and probably before then, since when he was younger and liked to rearrange my furniture for a laugh, I paid him as much attention as he deserved—little to none. Of course, he never had any luck, because... how do I put it?

He's a bit...odd. Touched. Full blown bonkers. Doesn't play well with others.

He did try to be a socialite, but humans don't find discussing wall moulds before diverging into the proper temperature at which to prime a cauldron as attractive as I do.

I was proud of him. About time he got a girlfriend and stopped moping about my halls getting dirty footprints everywhere. The stain on the drawing room carpet! Frightful!

I would miss the fun sessions of dance parties in my foyer, and prank wars where I rearranged all the rooms and left him to find his own way around—and boy, can Nick swear when he has to do a little work for a living—but it would be nice to have a girl around.

He brought her home to 'meet the parents' or rather, 'meet the House'. She stood in the entrance hall for a while running admiring hands over the paintings on my pillars with the proper amount of awe. I wagered she was from down at the village. She dressed like it. No one who can help it goes on a date wearing an apron and with their pretty, blonde hair all bundled up in a handkerchief like a cleaning lady.

He led her up to the kitchen, showed her around, and said some flattering things about how sophisticated and delicate I was and how I needed to be treated with respect. After the preliminaries, he proceeded to show her my cleaning closet where I keep all the mops and brooms for when I need to do a sprucing up. I pride myself on being the cleanest House this side of Îvâlte.

"I'm presuming you know your way around cleaning supplies?" Nicholas said.

*What is he up to?* Not for the first time, I wished he'd enchanted me up some arms. I could've slapped him. Much as I like being shown off, it was high time he wandered up to the north turret with his lady friend and had some fun. I'd set it all up the night before—fluffy pillows, a stash of chocolate, some of my ancient artefacts from the storerooms in the west wing to entertain them, even lit the fire so it would be cosy. All that work and he wanted to stand by the cleaning closet and talk brooms.

This is why he hadn't gotten a girlfriend in 400 years.

To get his attention, I rattled the door of the kitchen till the hinges gave an agitated squeak.

"One moment," he said, left the blonde, and strode a little way up the corridor. "What?"

"Why are you treating her like a cleaning lady?" I creaked via a loose floorboard. "Get a grip, man! You've got to romance her or she'll leave."

"She is the cleaning lady!" Nick's face contorted into an expression of bafflement.

"Cleaning lady?! We don't need a cleaning lady! I'm very clean!" A worrying crack zigzagged through the floorboard, and I calmed my voice before I broke something.

"Did you seriously think she was my girlfriend?" he said, laughing.

"You talked about her like she was," I creaked grumpily. "Next time try 'our new cleaning lady' instead of 'the new light of my life.'"

If you can believe it, he looked proud of himself for having tricked me. His eyes glittered with a disagreeable mix of amusement and triumph, and he returned to the broom closet with a step far too jaunty for my liking. Vexed, I morphed my corridor into a set of stairs instead. With a startled yelp, he tripped.

He made several satisfying thumps as he fell. The quiet once he reached the bottom was almost as satisfying. Served him right.

Into that quiet, before Nick had the chance to recover his scrambled wits enough to cuss me out, a laugh burst into existence, like a new-born flower.

There was Blondie, the new cleaning lady, who I'd rather forgotten about, standing on the other side of the hole in the floor where I'd conjured the stairs with a duster in one hand, laughing. She clutched at her stomach, tears streaming down her cheeks in her mirth, and I decided once and for all that I liked this one. Blondie would be staying. Permanently. And Nick could go lick my windows clean if he had a problem with that.

Which was a likely event, considering the stream of curse words echoing from the bottom of the stairs.

I gave Blondie the Sagebrush Room in the west wing, the best of my bedrooms, with the rose-patterned counterpane. Nick tried to send her home for the night, but I wasn't having that.

Thanks to his accidental tumble earlier, he had a fast growing lump on his head, bandaged nicely by our new friend from the village, and he didn't argue as much as he might have with that headache to remind him who was in charge here.

"You're being very disagreeable," he said, once we'd introduced Blondie to her new quarters. "We are not keeping Saoirse. She works once a week. She does not live in you."

Saoirse. She had a name. It didn't fit her. I preferred Blondie.

"She does now," I creaked back via a loose ceiling slat.

"If you push me down the stairs again I'll set your curtains on fire."

He wouldn't, and we both knew it, so I sat in smug silence as he grumbled his way to bed, and pulled the covers up over his eyes in an attempt to ignore me. As if he thought I'd be interested in him! Oh no, I was already preoccupied with boiling a pot of milk on my stove so I could bring Blondie a nice cup of cocoa and some biscuits before bed. She deserved it.

"You're very clean," Blondie said as she sought out dust bunnies along the mantelpiece in the White Parlour. "And you make very nice hot cocoa."

I thumped the books on the bookshelf nearby, pleased.

"You shouldn't have pushed Nick down the stairs yesterday," she added, her tone becoming disapproving, and she paused in her dusting to put her hands on her hips. "Though it was very funny. I hope you don't torment him like that often."

Indignant, I formed the pattern of the thumps into words.

"He torments me!"

She blinked, her dark eyes growing wide. "Did you just...talk?"

Nick chose that moment to stumble in, still in his dressing gown at one o'clock in the afternoon, with his hair mussed and the bandage sat at a jaunty angle across his forehead. "House," he said, waving one hand and gazing about in a bleary fashion, "I need that spell book on...Oh hello, Saoirse."

The change was laughable. One moment he's slouching around being his typical slobbish, lackadaisical self, the next he's pulled up straight, combing his hair flat, and dusting off his dressing gown.

So he did like her. Or he was at least capable of feeling some semblance of normal human emotion when faced with a pretty cleaning lady.

"Hello, Mister Wizard," she said, her lips twitching as she held back a laugh.

"Didn't realise you'd be in here," he said, scratching his head. "Can you clean somewhere else...?"

That did it. I knocked a book off the shelf onto him. It struck him between the shoulder blades—I was too nervous to hit him on the head again and potentially damage more brain cells. Heaven knows he's got them in short supply.

"Sorry to disturb you," he said, once he'd caught his breath. "House, let's take this into the corridor." He shot me a narrow-eyed look.

I took it into the corridor.

"House," he said, speaking slowly as if I were a small child, his arms crossed. "She is a cleaning lady. She is not a pet or a potential girlfriend."

"She could be all three," I pointed out, using another useful floorboard. I tried to keep one in each hallway for convenience's sake.

"Three in one. Think how useful that would be."

"No," Nick said in his most disagreeable voice, pinning me with his 'fearsome and powerful wizard' stare. Perhaps it would've been effective if he wasn't in a dressing gown with a bandage around his head.

"You like her. Come on," I creaked.

"I do not!" he protested, which further assured me that the opposite was true.

"Look, I'll make you dinner. Take her up to the north turret. I'll bring out some of those relationship building games. Give it a go."

"Definitely not."

"I could just deprive you of dinner unless you have it with her."

"I'll set your curtains on fire, and my bed sheets for good measure. Now I want that spellbook on transformations."

Creaking and groaning in complaint, I fetched the spellbook.

In the end, though, I got my way.

Nick and Blondie had dinner in the north turret.

Getting them alone together was all it took. Before long, they were joined at the hand, and after a few months, more often than not, joined at the lips too.

Humans. Why you think mushing your faces together is romantic is beyond me. You even have two kinds of face mushing—the one where you try and figure out what the other person had for dinner and the other kind where you smack heads as hard as you can to see whose skull cracks first. Nick and Blondie were getting well practised at the former. I only ever saw them have a skull cracking competition once.

Blondie stayed in the Sagebrush Room, and before long left my cleaning up to me again, since she had better things to do. Nick magicked her up dresses, jewellery and shoes. You name it, the girl got it.

"House, I'm taking Saoirse out for the day." Nick stood in the entrance hall with Blondie next to him. Both of them wore smart blue and silver outfits, and she looked delighted to be going out for a date. It was about time. He never took her anywhere.

I creaked a proud noise.

"See you later," the wizard said.

"Goodbye!" Blondie waved.

Of course, I didn't miss them. I spent an enjoyable day admiring the various artefacts in my storerooms, reshuffling my rooms and adding a few pretty accessories to Blondie's room. Not wanting Nick to feel left out, I dug up several old spellbooks I'd buried in a nook under the stairs and dumped them on the bed. He would've found them eventually but why not help him along. At dinner time, I heated up the kitchen stove and threw together a meal for them.

By midnight, they still weren't home.

I wasn't too bothered. When they really got going with the face-mushing and the goopy staring, they could lose track of time like nobody's business.

My front door clicked.

Nick slouched in, his outfit mud-spattered and a look of exhaustion on his face. I waited for Blondie, but she didn't come.

"Where's Blondie?" I asked as Nick shuffled to his bedroom. He ignored me, banging his door shut and flopping face down on his bed.

"Do you want dinner?"

No answer. Not an unheard of circumstance when he was sulking, but I'd never seen him lie *on top* of a stack of books before.

"Where's Saoirse?" I pressed, rattling the wardrobe doors.

My heartfelt concern earned a stream of angry cuss words, and he continued to lie face down on the books like the fool he was.

Had she dumped him? Or was he just having a tantrum?

She dumped him. It seemed more likely. Disappointing, but not entirely unexpected, I supposed. As I said, he truly does have the social-romantic skills of road kill, and village girls have the added blessing of getting picked up by handsome princes every so often. Wizards aren't really the sparkling, horse-riding heroes that make a good story, especially when they have lasting trauma from an encounter with broccoli soup and wear extra-large gold hoop earrings.

I removed the treats I'd found for Blondie from the shelf in her room. I wasn't bothered she was gone. Humans are so needy. It was probably a good thing. If she'd stayed, they might've decided to have more humans, and tiny humans are truly my worst nightmare. Sticky fingers everywhere…breaking everything…crying all the time…Ew.

Nick, overdramatic jilted wizard that he was, stayed flat on his face on his bed and did his level best to die. Of course, I wasn't having that, and after a few days, I tipped him out of bed. Repeatedly. It took five bed-tippings and subsequent climbing-back-ins before he got up and ate breakfast.

"Why did she dump you?" I couldn't help myself.

He shrugged a shoulder, stirring his soup. After two days pretending to be dead, he had the most impressive pasty skin and dark rings under his eyes.

"I dumped her," he said at last.

Enough was enough. I jolted the table and splashed soup on him.

"House!" he groaned, coughing and wiping bits of chicken and carrot off his face. "You know how stories work. The girl marries the prince, not the wizard. Stop spoiling things."

It took Blondie twenty years to think about things. She must've thought very hard, but she eventually came to a decision that she didn't like princes.

She reappeared on my doorstep. It was raining, water pouring out of the sky in great buckets. Being wet always makes me irritable—all that water in my crevices where it shouldn't be!—and I wasn't as glad to see her as I ought to have been.

"Took you long enough," I huffed to myself as I opened my door to let her in.

Nick hid under the stairs.

"Don't look so glum," I creaked to him. "It's not like she came back with a tiny human or something awkward."

He made a strangled noise and buried his head in his hands.

Meanwhile, Blondie dripped on my floor, her pretty hair all plastered to her face. Humans do even worse in wet weather than I do. Since Nick was a lost cause for the moment, I fetched a mop and bucket from a cupboard for her.

"Thank you, House," she said with a small smile, wringing out her hair and clothes into the bucket and mopping up the puddle she'd created.

Such a nice girl, that. With her busy, I turned my attention back to Nick, still huddled under the stairs, making tiny whimpering noises. What a failure.

"Why are you crying?" I rattled to him. "You're meant to be a powerful wizard. You can handle meeting your ex."

He raised his head enough to glare at me, but didn't comment. If anything, he bunched himself tighter into the gap under the stairs.

I love Nick. I really do. But he really is a stubborn little donkey of a man.

I took matters into my own walls.

"Go say hello." I tilted the floor, little by little, until he couldn't help but slide out from the crawl space. He crashed into Blondie's legs, and she yelped in surprise, tumbling over. The bucket wobbled, and out of fear of getting my tiles wet again, I righted the floor.

Nick and Blondie lay in an uncomfortable pile. She pushed herself up on her elbows, gazing into his face. He stared back, eyes wide.

Now. Face-mush. I waited.

"You got old," Nick said. Blondie slapped him.

I loved that woman so much.

Things had been so dull around here without her sudden bouts of rage.

"You left me!"

"Oops?" Nick offered, nursing his smarting cheek.

She looked like she'd slap him again, and I was all for it, but she decided against it, sitting back on her haunches instead.

"I walk here in the driving rain to speak to you and all you can say is oops? No apologies?"

"I never asked you to walk here in the rain," he said, his mouth turning down. "And the fact that it took you twenty years to argue the point makes me feel like a last resort."

Her face flushed hot red.

"You were always my first choice, you cursed wizard. You were the one who ditched me!"

I watched intently. This was intense. Humans. Always so emotional.

Nick frowned, opening his mouth to argue, and closing it again. He sounded remorseful when he whispered, "You could've done better."

"I've never heard so much rubbish in my life," Blondie said.

"It's not rubbish, it's..." He huffed out an agitated breath, glaring at her. "You're infuriating."

"I am. You're also rehiring me as cleaning lady."

"The House doesn't need..."

I cut him off with a well-placed creak, informing him that I did need a cleaning lady and I wasn't taking anyone other than Blondie. He shot me a look that suggested I would pay for it later, which I ignored.

Running a hand through his hair, he sighed, holding out a hand to her.

"Fine. Truce?"

She nodded.

"Truce."

They hugged. Maybe with a bit of face-mushing.

Not that I paid attention.

I was busy remaking Blondie's bed in the Sagebrush Room.

## ALLISON VANHUYSEN

---

## *The Resonance of the Zucchini*

M ovement is only effable in its absence. "You're to be on bedrest for the foreseeable future." Motion is only a desire when you can't have it.

"It'll be best for you and the baby to remain in the hospital so we can monitor the both of you."

The both of you. She'd always been a singular person, never a 'we', never a 'both'. Her independence was valuable, necessary. Her mother had warned her that a baby meant she would be tethered, stuck, but she thought she had three more months before all of that.

The baby was the barely size of a zucchini; how was it forcing her to surrender her freedom already?

"Oh sweetheart, oh, I'm here."

Oh no. She could speak to her mother, but in small doses, and with the capability to escape. Here? She was totally and completely stuck. Trapped by the Zucchini. Lovely.

She had tried a meditation app (one of the cheap, app-store recommended ones) a while ago to try and diminish the frequency of the escapes. It didn't help much. The only useful thing about it was the breathing routine; in, hold, out, hold. Again and again, until the need for sovereignty dissipated.

"They call this a maternity room? This is hardly fit for civilization! There is absolutely, positively nothing on these walls! And they make you wash your hands in those giant tubes?! It's unimaginable; I'll have to visit my granddaughter in a jail cell!"

Breathe, hold, release, hold.

"It is a granddaughter, right? Your brother's sure to have a whole brood of little boys, what with all the sports he plays. You're my only shot at a little granddaughter! Oh, and did I tell you about your brother's soccer? His rec league got spotted. He's going to try out for the Cavaliers!"

Breathe, hold, release, hold.

Growing up, her brother was untouchable. Soccer had been his religion- he worshiped early mornings and late nights, and dragged the family to his church on the weekends. She, on the other hand, devoted herself to academics. Started work at the end of eighth grade—part time at the diner down the street, part time filling out scholarship applications. It worked out. She put herself through college, took internships in the summers, and landed her dream job as a marketing consultant for a company organizing international education. But her brother, with his rec leagues and his Athletic Training Company? He got to actually move. She travelled to all of these cities and countries and cultures for her job, but in the end, she was stuck on bedrest. Motionless.

"When the baby comes I want to throw a party, sort of like a Post-Birth Baby Shower... (She stops to glare at me here, as if my being admitted to the hospital was very detrimental to her Baby Shower Planning)... I want my little granddaughter to have all of the love, and adoration she deserves from the community!"

The thought of that sends her spiralling out of her breathing methods. The Zucchini, passed around by the grandmothers of the Rotary club, with her pleading with them to please support the head. The Zucchini around all of her cousin's kids, running wildly around the living room. Her mother, lowering her voice to explain the absence of the father.

In, out, in, out.

She can't pause in between anymore; the breaths are coming fast and anxious. Her nervousness is almost palpable in the ions charging through the room. The room feels small and cramped, and she wants to hug my knees, but her belly's too big, and everything just seems so ridiculously out of control, and foreign. The monitor starts to beep with her elevated heart rate, and she immediately feels guilty. The nurses are already understaffed, and so many people in the maternity ward need them much more than she does. They're dealing with much more than her mother's premature party planning.

"Is everything OK in here? Your heart rate seems to be a bit more elevated than usual?"

The nurse is one of those people who end everything with a question mark, as if she's unsure of her very thoughts. Her mother is not one of those people.

"Oh, she's completely fine. Just got a bit too excited about her Baby Shower is all…"

Even with her mother's reassurance, the nurse checks her vitals and does a basic checkup. Apparently 'overly enthusiastic' is not a viable medical diagnosis. The nurse seems to be a bit overly enthusiastic herself. She'd been here for the entirety of her stay, smiling at patients and doing various 'Maternity Nurse' duties. Every day during her lunch break she walked through the halls, waving at the patients. She had thought the nurse's walk was a bit odd, one step smooth, the other bounced. She watched this with a sort of odd fascination, this graceful bounced gait. Motion had become an obsession; she watched the way people moved now. The mothers wheeled out, the hiss of the chairs against the faded pale tiles. Her mother's hip swinging, going-nowhere amble. Movement paces in circles around her, never stopping, while she lies in the plastic-rimmed hospital bed, she and the Zucchini motionless.

"So, honey, are you sure about all this? I mean, all you did was decide by yourself, and then you just walked right into that clinic… Are you really, totally, completely sure? This isn't something you do lightly, you know?"

She's thirty-one, single, and completely stable. She's done the math; it seems to be the right time from any angle. She's young enough so that it's not yet considered geriatric. She's at a point in her career where she's able to take maternity leave. She figures this will be a good filter out for guys too: if they don't like the Zucchini, she won't like them. Simple math.

"Honey. You've explained your standpoint to me a million times over, but are you really ready for the actual baby? They're a lot of work, the toll it takes on your body, and then there's the absence of the father, what will you do? How are you going to balance your work with this child?"

She acts like the Zucchini isn't already in existence. It's been a child—her baby—since the time she walked into that clinic. It wasn't one of those sketchy things you see in the movies, it exuded a feeling of cleanliness. She flipped through the pages—the motion didn't seem to fit the enormity of the action. Forget her high school romance, the bad first dates, her brief jaunt into online dating. She picked genetics and achievements over romance, because it wasn't about her. It was about the child.

"So, honey, can you tell me who the father is? The girls at my book club were telling me about a girl who told everybody she went to the sperm bank, but when the baby popped out it looked exactly like the next door neighbour! I'm not in for anything unexpected, right?"

The dad's name was William J. Stergstate. He played tennis, had a Labrador, a happy (if extended) family, no history of genetically transmitted disease. Ninety-five percent Polish, five percent French, attributing to wavy dark hair and blue-gray eyes. Sperm that will most likely not result in a baby who could stunt double the doctor with the receding hairline who lives in the apartment next door.

"So, will you ever meet the father?"

That was the plan. She followed him on Facebook, but his account hadn't been updated in three years. She even messaged him—no response of course. She found his mother under the follower's list. Her account hadn't been used in three years either, her last post was an obituary. So, no. She will never meet the father. His mother, on the other hand? She was on her way to the hospital right now.

"Did I tell you about my new pickleball league? They opened this huge gym down the street, and they have all of these courts! I'm scheduled to play in thirty minutes, so I'm going to have to leave you soon, sweetie."

Oh, thank goodness. She loved her mother, but she was a bit much sometimes. She was an expert at talking—listening? Not so much... She wanted to listen, she wanted to hear what happened, to actually connect with somebody on HIS side; somebody to tell her if she was making a huge mistake.

There wasn't anything to do but watch in the hospital. Out the window there was just a street framed by apartment buildings. The hallway was her only other option; pregnant women pushed furiously to the delivery center, the bouncing nurse passing occasionally; the motivational posters hanging on the drab walls. An older woman wheeling steadily down the corridor.

"Is this room 318? I'm looking for my son's... Well, I'm not really sure what to call her..."

So, this was her. Pale blue jumpsuit, ashy gray hair twisted up into a vaguely European chignon. Strong jawline balanced by delicate cheekbones, gray eyes edged with smile lines. She looked like a quintessential retired school teacher. Did she know that her grandkid was the size of a zucchini? How many grandkids did she have? How many has she met?

"I've never done this before. I didn't even know that he had donated until after the accident. You're the first one since. I didn't expect any of this to go this way."

She waves her hand fluidly down at her chair.

"There was an accident, you know. He was driving us home. The driver hit us on his side. My legs were crushed under the right side of the dashboard—the airbag on his side never deployed. The wheel hit him in the chest. He couldn't breathe. He pushed me out of the car—the EMTs tried to revive him but couldn't. I was trapped, motionless on that stretcher while they worked over him. I was trapped when they stopped. The worst feeling is the lack of movement, isn't it?"

Yes. Yes, it is. People start moving around by the time they're a Zucchini. To limit that, or stop that, it's shattering. Standing still, holding tight, being trapped; it goes against the basic makeup of humanity. Motion goes on around while people are stuck. The world spins with wheelchair tyres. It seems like an inherent right until it stops.

Movement is only effable in its absence. Motion is only a desire when you can't have it.

The drab little room. The window and the hallway. The elegant lady in the wheelchair hovering a safe distance. The girl in the bed with her hands on her stomach. The Zucchini in her stomach, kicking for the first time.

Motion.

# STEVEN JACKSON

---

# *A Static Hero*

"It's true, you know. You can google it," said Harris, the Geography NQT, imperiously. "If a shark stops swimming, it dies."

Harris's more senior colleague in the Geography Department, Mrs Milton, bespectacled and becardiganed in the style of a matronly librarian, was sitting next to him in one of the well-worn leather armchairs at the far end of the staffroom. She ceased sipping her tea and nodded maternally at him. She had been listening to Mr Harris ever since he'd sat down beside her and started waxing lyrical about Shark Week on the Discovery Channel.

"It's to do with their gills," he added.

"I see. How interesting..."

"It is, isn't it?"

"Very..."

It was the last week of the Trinity Term and the whole school faculty were congregating in the staffroom that morning for the headmaster's final address of the academic year.

In the far left corner as you went in, by the bookcases, there were the three aspiring professors, all doctorates, discoursing about football and existentialism; in the far right corner by the bay windows that looked out onto the playing fields, there was an earnest group of self-important, serious-frowning pedagogues already in discussion about timetabling issues for next September; the younger generation of teachers, the 'newbies', with their water bottles and laptops, were sheepishly piled up by the fire exit, as if still unsure about their invitation to the party; the 'old hats', the seasoned teachers, ostentatiously complacent, were lounging together in their safe circles on the familiar sofas in the middle; and those at the top of the tree—the Senior Leadership Team—were positioned at the front, by the pigeonholes, by the big meeting bell, sharing in whispers all manner of classified information too important to be disclosed to the unexpectant mob before them.

One figure sat apart. He was positioned at the back just off from Harris and Milton. An old man. He had a large domed head, heavy looking, which sunk a little between his shoulders. He sat ponderously, as if there was some higher, philosophical truth woven into the pattern of the shag rug at his feet. He was the only one in the room that knew that the word 'shag' in this instance was derived from the Old English word *sceacga*, which was closely related to the Old Norse word *skeg*, which meant *beard*. He was the only one in the room that knew that a shag rug is called a shag rug because it is shaggy like a beard—not because you shag on it.

Dr Alfred E. Byrd. He taught English. He'd been at Wainwright's College for thirty-three years. He'd once been Head of Department. He wasn't now.

He was distinguished, however. He had thick, white hair, curly like Aeschylus, pushed back from the brows. His little bald spot was unnoticeable. He wore a silk tie, modestly; a firm collar, buttoned up to the chin.

He always wore the same lapel pin. It was a miniature coat of arms. Those colleagues that took notice simply assumed it was an old public school badge or a family crest. One bright History teacher, who'd examined it a little more closely, once remarked to the others that it looked like something to do with Henry V: that it was something a person might buy for a fiver from a giftshop in Stratford-upon-Avon. People laughed at the joke.

And it could be argued that the heraldic design on Dr Byrd's pin was a bit like Henry V's. After all, it was a crest, like Henry's, in quarters of opposing red and blue (although, for Dr Byrd, 'of opposing gules and azure' would have been more precise). And, yes, two of the quarters were bedecked with lilies, just like Henry's (though, again, Dr Byrd might have innocently pointed out that Henry's *fleurs-de-lis* were gold, not white like his own, and positioned on the red quadrants, not the blue).

But there was one giant difference that would have had to have been noted. Most importantly, *unlike* Henry's, there were no golden lions on the crest of Dr Byrd's pin. Just the single white pelicans of piety associated with the academic institution in which Dr Byrd had undertaken his formative undergraduate studies: Corpus Christi College, Cambridge. If only Dr Byrd had been privy to the bright History teacher's joke at the time and able to proffer a riposte, they all could have had a laugh at his lapel pin together.

At last, the headmaster, Mr Dixon, entered, *in medias res,* with the Deputy Head Academic, Ms Snout, by his side. Dixon, a wire-thin and surprisingly short man, who rarely outstripped the taller eleven-year-olds at the school, as ever, was dressed in a slick, pinstripe suit. He positioned himself deliberately at the front of the room and, for a moment, allowed the general chatter to continue. He stood, arms folded, observing the natural behaviours and interactions of the creatures before him, the way one might when observing the animals at the zoo.

When wholly satisfied that enough was enough, he nodded curtly to his personal secretary, Susan, who had her hand ready-poised on the pendulous clapper of the meeting bell, and at that, she jiggled back and forth the big brass teat so energetically that the resounding alarum emitted from her tiny fist sent a shockwave through the room. It was immediately and universally accepted as a sign for hush.

"Thank you. Thank you," Dixon began. "Welcome, all, to this our final briefing. And how should I begin? Shall I start by stating that this academic year has been a success overall? Yes, I think I shall. It was only back in September—if some of you can remember that long ago…" Here, Dixon paused dramatically and scanned the faces of his faculty in mock scrutiny, as if making considered judgements on their separate mental capacities.

"…Yes, it was only ten months ago that we started in such fine style. Our student population was the biggest in Wainwright's history; our first form intake was unprecedented. We had more student bums on classroom seats in Year 7 than ever before. Imagine that."

The panel of approving SLT members nodded in unison at this, while a majority of the general teachers were left wincing at the reference to student bums. Dr Byrd wore a more puzzled expression, however, as he began considering more appropriate and aesthetic examples of synecdoche, which the headmaster might have used for capturing the pupil-collective-body of the school.

"And as the year unfolded we saw further firsts and even better records smashed. Eighty-per-cent of our sixth formers were given conditional offers to red brick universities and fifteen of that cohort attended Oxbridge interviews, no less. By Easter we were delighted to discover that a record seven—I repeat, SE-VEN—of our students had been accepted to either Oxford or Cambridge, A-Level results depending... Magdalen and Balliol, Pembroke, the Queen's and Corpus Christi will become the academic homes of our alumni. Jesus and Christ's too!" Dr Byrd's eyes lifted from the shag rug for the first time and he looked up at the mention of his old college. It was his student, Anthony Hardwick—a Marlowe obsessive—who was off to read English at Corpus Christi in September.

He stared out of the bay windows at the green fields, which opened and unfurled to the thick, dark wall of unending fir trees, skirting the school grounds.

The headmaster's speech continued but the words soon became an incoherent drone to Dr Byrd's ear, then phased out entirely. He was trying to imagine the horizon without that great backdrop of trees. He was trying to picture the moment in time when the firs had not existed in such permanent, towering form. But they were fixed now—a distinguishing feature of the school campus—unmoving sentinels, guarding the edges of the site, semiotically suggesting that the patch of land and the world within were safely contained and demarked. Those trees, Dr Byrd considered, like the timber and the stone and the bricks of the buildings, formed part of the material fabric of the school. They were vital, like any other part of the institution. Vital. Just like the chapel, the old library, or the recently-built science centre. Vital, like the people: those long-gone, those current, those passing through, and those soon to be welcomed in. The pupils, the teachers, the alumni, the headmasters and headmistresses, the governors, the groundskeepers, the secretaries, the cooks and the cleaners...

Timeless. Enduring. Not time-bound, but bound up in time. Living its own history, its own present, perpetually entering into its own future. A great moving wheel. A school.

Would Wainwright's College still be Wainwright's College

without those trees, he thought.

He felled the lot of them in his mind with one God-like stroke, cleared the horizon of sheltering trees entirely, and a hallowed light flooded the scene, blessing the fields with gold...

"Dr Byrd?"

Dixon's voice suddenly became discernible. "Dr Byrd? Would you care to say a few words?"

Dr Byrd turned slowly in his seat and realised that everyone was looking at him, for the headmaster had just announced to the room another record for the school: that, after the longest known teaching service in Wainwright's history—'an unrivalled period of thirty-three years, no less'—the eminent and esteemed, Dr Byrd, was retiring at the end of the term, and that this week was to be his last in the profession. There was something close to a reverent silence in the room, as Dr Byrd cleared his throat to speak. He did not stand, but remained sitting. He did not look up.

"Well, thank you, Headmaster, but I've really not much to say..."

A disappointed murmur was audible.

Dr Byrd was tired. He thought for some seconds, searching for words, and cleared his throat again.

"No...I would like to say that, for a long time, I have believed that the nature of us all—the nature of school life, in particular—consists entirely of progress and motion. Yes, momentum is a blessed thing, and to be swept along with it is a joy. I see us now, as members of this school, coasting gloriously, like dolphins or mermaids, singing to each other, riding seawards on the waves, combing the surf of the present moment. And I have started to understand that anything static or unmoving is not for this life—not for this institution. I've been teaching here for thirty-three years. Some might consider that a grand thing. Others might view it as a period of unadventurous stasis. Regardless, a static hero will, one day, become a liability..."

Dr Byrd trailed off, smiling at the image.

There was silence again. It endured. Dr Byrd was seemingly done. No one knew what to do. Did they all clap now? They were in desperate need of direction.

"Er...and what will you do next?' Dixon asked finally, trying to glean some sort of satisfactory clarity from the enigmatic old man, for the sake of the general persons present.

"I'll buy a pair of white flannel trousers and eat peaches on the beach," Dr Byrd responded instantly.

All was saved. The room burst into laughter, not entirely knowing why.

Dixon delivered the last, more general valedictory remarks to his staff and as people began to leave, going their separate ways, back to respective department offices, off to teach first lessons and their awaiting classes, the atmosphere in the room quickly dissolved into something more prosaic.

Dr Byrd shuffled quietly away, navigating the gauntlet of handshakes, niceties and fond farewells as he went.

Some of the lucky few who were not teaching first period, remained behind. Mrs Milton fetched another cup of tea and a couple of biscuits. Harris did the same.

"How interesting," she mused, munching through a rich tea finger. "I never saw that one coming."

"What's that?" said Harris.

"I never saw it coming. The old bird."

"Who?" said Harris.

"Dr Byrd."

"Oh."

"Been here forever."

"Has he?"

"Thirty-odd years."

"That's long."

"Can you imagine?" said Mrs Milton, dunking another biscuit.

"No way," declared Harris. "You'd never get me stuck in one place for too long. That's for sure."

ANNA LINSTRUM

---

# *Untethered*

Along the edge of one door was a faded red, white and blue stripe and the peeling silhouette of a surfer. A slogan missing three letters had once urged: *One Life, Live It.*

Curled up inside, she'd positioned herself so that all she could see was the porcelain sky, with only the occasional high puff of cloud to interrupt the glassy blue. They trundled, rumbling over asphalt, the familiar rattle of the wheel arch a constant companion. Infrequently, the tops of some trees sped along the base of the window frame, suggesting life at their roots: fences, farms, turnings, gateposts. But mostly it was sky, passing without seeming to pass, changing, yet always the same.

The labourer they bought it from it from was a blow-in too, like them. He lived in the mountains a few miles from the stifling city in a one-storey pink stucco cabaña with chickens outside and some neighbours three metres away, though there was nothing else for miles around. He was as gnarled and rusty as the van, and seemed to feel such an immediate affinity with them that he didn't even bother to put a shirt on, so Nina was left feeling obscurely uncomfortable with his naked skin as he showed them round the vehicle. He loved this country, he said, sunshine all year, away from 'all that crap'. *There's crap everywhere*, said Tam, but the man was walking away.

Up in the driver's seat, Tam suddenly turned the radio up loudly to a local station. Before leaving, Nina had chosen music for the old cassette deck, but after three months travelling the familiar tunes rattled round the cavity of the vehicle like dry beans, offering little nourishment.

We're too old for this, she thought, as she shifted her lower back on the lumpy mattress and turned her head to squint out of the other side. It was the same as the first. They'd had a row about macaroni around forty kilometres ago and she'd decided to feign sleep rather than say anything else on the subject of pasta.

She felt the van lurch to the right and the clear sky was suddenly segmented into trees and poles much closer to the window, followed by the corner of a sign. She pulled the grubby duvet over her head, her torso rocking gently left and right as the van turned corners. After a bit it slowed right down, reversed cautiously then went forward one final time before jerking to a stop.

*Nina*? said Tam. She could tell from his voice that he'd turned to look over his shoulder into the back. She didn't respond. She heard him climb out and slam the door. A few seconds later she felt the sound of the petrol cap being opened and the nozzle being shoved in. The hum of the pump. She peeped from under her cover, face hot. She could see Tam's cheek, his eyes fixed on the numbers as they spun upwards. Man's work, she thought. That's how they see it.

The clonk-click of the nozzle hooking back onto the pump. The snap of the petrol cap closing. Tam's head disappearing from view.

She creaked her aching body to a sitting position, her gaze landing on the petrol pump. She hadn't thought much about what they'd do when they got back. She had supposed they'd resume work in the stifling city, get their apartment back, but it suddenly struck her that this wasn't necessarily going to be the case. Her mind handled this thought warily, not liking to look. One thing was clear: the idea of going back to what everyone else considered their home country was alarming, a country they'd not lived in for years, a country that felt less and less welcoming and more and more like a shifting deck of cards, superficially full of endless variants yet flipping over the same jacks and queens, dealing the same petty squabbles and the same mean and selfish habits time and again.

She shifted her bottom on the mattress and craned her neck to see where Tam had gone. A short distance from the petrol pumps was a small squat building that said *Speedy-Snak* in blue and yellow neon, alongside a copse of pine trees and some picnic benches. A family was packing up their breakfast into boxes and rucksacks, moving with unhurried, well practised movements. They had neat gear and tasteful clothes, so Nina decided they were Dutch.

The smallest child, a boy of about five, was with some difficulty, attempting to slot drinks bottles into a camping case, but the circular fabric openings were frustrating him. Every time he pulled one wide to accept the bottom of the bottle it would fold shut when he let go. With each attempt, he realigned the camping case between his legs and shifted his bottom, to try for a better purchase, which efforts were causing him to turn in a slow circle on the grass. Nina became absorbed in this miniature drama, willing the boy to succeed. The father leant over to say something and was batted away by a small star-shaped hand, she saw the mouth pucker and the chin lift—no, she thought, he wants to do it himself. Eventually, using his chin as a vice, he managed to hold an opening wide, and slotted his first bottle in. The four other members of the family were now standing around watching, their tasks finished; an older child made as if to help, but the mother put a hand on his shoulder. The little boy was now managing the final bottle with less difficulty, his whole body and full concentration involved in his challenge. As it went in, he turned instantly with a wide smile, the family burst into applause and his lanky father bent to give him a small kiss on the top of his head. The mother scooped the little boy up in her arms and he buried his face in her soft caramel hair. Nina absently lifted a hand to touch her own, thick and black, needing a wash and tangled almost into a dreadlock at the back. She watched the parents bustle their tanned offspring into a gaggle and stride away from the picnic area, feeling oddly bereft.

Suddenly realising she needed a wee, she galvanised into action and cast about for her flip flops, Tam would be back so she needed to hurry. Unable to locate them she shoved some blue woollen socks on her feet instead and, leaving the duvet in a heap, she opened the back door and padded out. The concrete felt cool under the awning, then immediately baking hot through her blue socks as she left its shade. She hurried over to the *Speedy-Snak* and up the slight slope to the double doors. Once inside, the interior was blissfully air-conditioned and had the familiar odour of foreign supermarkets—coffee, baguette, sweets, underscored with cleaning fluid and plastic packaging.

The toilet was spotless, which was just as well, since she was regretting not hunting for her flip flops more thoroughly under the mess of the van, but she couldn't have stood another sarcastic comment from Tam about losing things, or making him wait, or maybe having thought about needing a wee sooner.

As she was washing her hands a man came in with a bucket and mop. He was dark and black-haired, of indeterminate age, with a thin face and eyes that were large and wary and which opened almost in alarm on seeing her. *Pardonez-moi*, he said hastily. *Pas de problème,* she said, *Vas-y.*

She continued at the sink and after a few seconds of hesitation, he pushed open one of the cubicles with his foot and started to mop the floor.

*Salut*, she said lightly as she left, but he didn't respond.

She passed a tiny shop on her way back, nothing more than carousels and stands, piled with luminous and mysterious shapes encased in netting to entice children. At one end was a rack advertising maps, which reminded her she'd ruined one of theirs by accidentally dangling the corner of it in a fire and then chucking Tam's beer over it in an attempt to douse the flames. All the maps were muddled and it took an age to sort through them, but when she'd finally found the correct one, she remembered she didn't have any money. Berating herself for being the utter flake that Tam said she was—*I've a degree in political science*, she'd reply hotly, and he would say something intended to be charming but which would sting anyway, like, *Sure an' but politics have changed since those times, eh?*—she opened the door of the *Speedy-Snak*, padded down the slope in her thick dirty socks and realised with a jolt that the van was no longer there.

She took a couple of steps forward, as if it might reappear like a mirage when she shifted. When it didn't, her head flicked to the left, to the right. Her steps faltered into the burning sunlight, her palm went up to shield her eyes and she felt a rush of relief as the thought came: *tyre pressure, water, those things.* Her alarm easing, she padded all the way along the front of the building, past the windows of the tiny café that lay at the far end, and rounded the corner to look down the side. Scrubby, dry plants and a thin littered strip was all that met her eyes. She hurried back along the building to the other side, but it was simply more scrub and a grassy bank that eventually ran down to the motorway. She spun round now, scouring the edges of things, walls, trees, corners, trying to look behind and over as if she might conjure up a vehicle from the margins by the simple act of looking. The air and water tanks, she noticed now with a sickening lurch, stood in solitary commune a small distance from where she'd last seen it.

She told herself not to panic, that it was a momentary blip, a crease that would be pressed smooth again, yet the thought now of their van, with its familiar rattles and the red, white and blue stripe down the side of one door, was sending a swift and powerful surge of yearning through her body; this van that had felt like a cell only fifteen minutes ago was now the refuge and the comfort, the only home in a probably hostile and certainly reckless world. Unbelievably, incredibly, it had been spirited out of her reach.

He'll come back, she thought, when he notices I'm not there. She thought of the tumbled duvet in the back. A cursory glance in the rear-view mirror from the driver might naturally assume a person was still underneath.

Unless.

No. That was madness.

No, because when he'd cooled off, forgotten about the macaroni and the music, he'd call her name, louder, louder, more urgently, he'd stop the van and check the duvet, move into rescue mode and screech the van round the next roundabout and hurtle back, that's what would happen. Her brain whirred...the services was on this side of the carriageway, he'd have to drive all the way back down the other side to the previous junction, she frantically tried to imagine how far away that had been, she turned to face the motorway, trying to remember, but realising she hadn't been paying attention enough to have the faintest idea how long it might take him and that anyway all speculation was ultimately pointless.

A fresh swell of misery engulfed her at the thought of her shoes buried somewhere in the mess inside. The shoes somehow made her feel worse. Despite the heat, a film of cold sweat insinuated itself across her chest.

She crossed to the picnic table and sat on the bench.

Think, Nina, think. Think.

I think.

Can I walk somewhere? No, where on earth to?

Think again.

Can I make a phone call? No, I've no money. And who would I ring?

I think about the limited contact with home. Three phone calls made in unsavoury public telephone boxes, one to Tam's mother who had threatened to unleash any number of unholy furies and throw the *Old Testament* at his head if he didn't phone her at least once to alert her to his not being dead in a ditch, one to the neighbour in the city who'd promised to keep an eye on the flat, and a third to the water company, because the neighbour said they'd visited the building and tried to cut the supply.

I sit on the picnic bench in my socks. My right knee begins to jiggle up and down. He'll be back. I just need to wait.

A single potato crisp, crinkly and yellow, sits on the grass, a small piece of the breakfast scene. I crush it with my toe and through my sock I can feel the crisp break. At the thought of the Dutch family, I start to cry.

A while later, embarrassed by the disapproving glances thrown at the unkempt woman taking up a whole picnic table, I retreat to the grass and pretend to enjoy the sun, tilting my head to its heat.

After the lunchtime rush, I return to the bench.

The sun is setting. A thin dagger of light has found the gap between the building and the pine trees, narrowing to a point on the ground. The neon blue and yellow of the *Speedy-Snak* sign is more vivid, the lights inside growing sickly and luminous; the distant headlights push through the darkening day. A breeze stirs the branches and I awake with my neck stiff and a crease on my cheek from the fabric of my shirt.

A man is standing next to me. I jolt upright. It's the man from the toilets. He still has his blue and yellow uniform on, a little cap on his head to denote the people who pay him. He holds out his hand. In it there is small wrapped chocolate bar.

*T'as faim, no*? His French is heavily accented. At that moment I realise I am in fact ravenous, and so I take it.

*Merci*, I say.

*T'Algerie*? he asks, briskly. His chin jabs up, as if indicating my person, something about me, and I'm confused at first, then realise he means the way I look. I shake my head. I'm about to tell him the country I'm from, but it sticks to my tongue, refusing to be named. Uncomfortable. Unwieldy.

Then he speaks again.

*You are lost?*

I think for a moment.

*Yes,* I say.

He sits next to me and gets another chocolate bar out of his pocket which he starts to eat.

*I am Rafik,* he says.

*Nina*, I say.

He has to clean the toilets one more time before he can go home. When I ask him what he did before this, he seems reluctant to say. The sun has dropped down behind the horizon and a chill is at our backs from the trees.

He lives with two women, he says, *over there*, gesturing vaguely, the women are his friends, they are not French either, but they share common needs and they like to sit and eat together, talk of their day, of their families back home. When I ask him if he wants to go back he says, *but of course*. As if I was a mad woman to ask this question. And he tells me about it. He tells me about his home and his family, his mother, her soft eyes, her hand stirring a pot, her arms sweeping up children, grandchildren, smoothing clothes and tablecloths, slapping dough on a surface, smiling. And I feel no fear at being sat here with this strange man with large eyes and a chocolate bar for his dinner. The chocolate is a perk of the job of cleaning up other people's mess, but he's supposed to bring his own supper and eat it in a tiny cupboard they call a Staff Rest Room. They don't let him eat a meal at the picnic tables.

*So, I prefer chocolate bar out here, with the trees,* he says. He holds up the last piece, with a raisin sticking out of it. *This they call a break,* he says, popping it in his mouth and crunching the wrapper with his other hand. *So is OK next to trees.*

This seems unfair, and I say so. *This is why you are so thin*, I add. And he nods, sadly, but then smiles too, a twinkle at the corner of his eye, and he pats his tummy. Then: *University*, he says. *This is where I work, at home. But regime does not like my teaching.*

*Aha!* I say, *Regime doesn't much like me either,* and he laughs, a bark of recognition and he says, *They do not like what they cannot measure.*

He stands, holds out his hand for my silver wrapper, taking it to the bin along with his own. He looks at his watch, a large digital one with a thick strap, like a mountaineer. *One more clean,* he says.

An hour later and it is quite dark now. All I can see of the traffic are the headlights and what is caught in them. Each time a car turns in to get petrol the beam sweeps across the picnic tables and reveals the lone figure of a woman in her socks. No one comes over to ask if I'm OK.

Raf wheels a pushbike over to the bench.

*Toilets done. You cannot stay here. Is not nice.*

And Nina feels no qualm at all about getting on the back of his bike. The night air cloaks her body softly, her lungs breath it deeply in, this gentle freshness. Raf stands up to pedal, allowing her to sit on the saddle. Her feet in their thick blue woollen socks hang down either side of the back tyre.

*Is not far,* he says, before adding, *I good cook.*

And he sets off down the side of the concrete building, then swings sharply right, taking a narrow path she hadn't noticed before. This path skirts along the side of the pine trees, which reveal themselves to be not the copse she had assumed, but the corner of a large, majestic forest. She bumps along on the saddle as he pedals over the dry path. Abruptly it switches to smooth black tarmac, allowing the rubber tyres to glide with a gentle, crackling sound over its surface, whispering into the night.

Her hair lifts gently from her forehead and the stars wink.

*Over there,* he says, lifting one hand to point ahead to a village, a town, Nina can't tell which, but as she follows his hand, she sees that there are lights twinkling from dwellings and that the very last of the sun is catching the low clouds in a brilliant streak of amber and gold.

Just as the red light of Raf's bike flickers and vanishes down the side of the forest, the headlights of a battered van with red, white and blue down the side of one door and the peeling remains of an urgent slogan swing into the petrol station, the beam slipping across the base of the trees.

The van sweeps round slowly and comes to a stop in front of the deserted picnic table. The driver's door opens. A man steps out and looks around. The wind whispers through the pines, the only sound over the low rumble of the motorway. A silver wrapper sticks out from the mess of the rubbish bin, but the man does not see it, for why would he, why would he see this, as he stands, alone, the yellow and blue neon sign of the *Speedy-Snak* a virulent rebuke, blurting across the moonlit night?

ASHIA MIRZA

# *Yahya's Garden*

It was the night he collected the snails and slugs in a green plastic bucket and took them to the woods that he noticed me.

"Hello, is someone there?"

I could have stayed as the sapling. Or taken the shape of a squirrel, an owl or a fox. Instead, I walked out of the thicket in the form of our ancestors. Dark hair, as lush as the leaves around me. Skin the colour of the dark earth I grew out of. The soil was older than any of the ancient trees. I created a figure that I knew would please him.

Mother wouldn't be happy.

His startled eyes fell on my breasts with an evolutionary urge.

I could have used sorcery, but I trusted fate instead. Another thing Mother detested.

"Are you OK? Are you hurt?" he asked.

"I'm lost," I said.

He pulled his jacket off and wrapped it loosely around my shoulders. It felt like a kite stuck in the tree; plastic debris abandoned in the woods; a dog-poo bag hanging off a branch. I suppressed the shudder to shake it off me, the same way that a human flicks a spider off their shoulder or a fly off their arm.

"Shall I call the police?"

"No."

"Is there anyone else I can call?"

"No."

Maybe it was the desperate swiftness of my reply, but his whole composure changed.

"There's a refuge not far from here. I can take you there?" It took me a moment to realise he was referring to the places where beaten human women stay.

"No."

He shuffled his feet and scratched the back of his head.

"Well...er...I came here to bring these fellers." He picked out the slugs and snails one by one and placed them down on the grass. "You're welcome to come back to mine...if you want to, that is...and you can clean up and use my phone." He said it in a way that was settled.

He was always better at making decisions than I was.

Maybe that was why I stayed with him.

Everything seemed so much easier. My head emptied of the heavy balls of clay soil. I captured the energy of the sunlight, and my veins carried the photosynthetic sweetness to my soul.

The neighbours weren't happy with my nakedness, so I wore the clothes he chose made from wool, flax, silk and cotton when I went outside. Materials that didn't feel like an itchy fungus on my skin. And I covered myself in a robe when I answered the door after that day when he found the postman frozen with his mouth open and a package in his hand.

I tended to his crops. Year after year, he was delighted with his harvest of leeks, beans, onions, cucumber and courgettes. He said I had green fingers and laughed when I made them so. Somehow, I knew he didn't want me to tell him that I'd helped them grow healthy and large with enchanted words and a magical touch. That I'd murmured a spell over the slugs and other garden pests, so they left the garden. He didn't like me interfering with his tomatoes, though; he said it was the first thing he'd ever grown and didn't want to lose his touch.

We cooked meals I didn't need because I could absorb nutrients from the ground. But I ate with him, and it reminded me of the feast days I'd loved as a child.

I was different, but he accepted it.

Mother never had.

For eight years, my heart beat as carefree as an infant.

I walked to the spot where we had first met and examined a spherical bunch of rooted dandelion souls. Each floret cast its own euphoric light that danced across my face, and my insides glowed with the energy created.

A young boy came running, trampling many others and stopped next to my cluster. His mouth hung open, and his moody brown eyes grew as wide as the composite flower heads. He looked into my face, and I smiled with understanding. Maybe he saw what I did.

A frenzy of boyhood swept over him, and his face contorted as though it was melting in the sun. He turned and kicked the clump over and over. All the dandelion heads scattered.

His mother pushed a pram over the bereft stems, and it veered towards the army of out-of-control nettles that grew alongside a narrow, stone path. Her right hand held a phone in front of her artificially tanned face. Fake lashes curled up like a Venus flytrap about to snap on her dark, high-arched eyebrows.

Sunset-yellow petals stuck to the thick tyres.

Spinning round.

Dazed. Dying. Dead.

The baby screamed an elegy when the nettles brushed along her legs.

Time stopped.

I picked up a nearby dandelion clock.

I whispered across it and blew.

The white parachutes surfed my breath of life.

Beneath my feet, I felt the long taproot dance. The root that clones when divided. That would grow from a fragment and bring back life.

Mother rose out of my garden the next day, as tall as the sunflowers around her. Her face and body were the colour of the destroyed dandelion roots. She trampled dirt into my kitchen, and my bare feet absorbed it like a warm sea breeze.

When the kettle boiled, her vine arm extended forwards and poured the water into a mug. She grew an extra twig, snapped it off, dipped it into the water and tasted it. It reminded me of when Yahya used to dunk chocolate fingers in his tea.

"Girl, I taste good!" She put the root back in the water, pulled some petals off her hair and put those in too. She pushed the drink towards me.

I sipped the nutritious infusion whilst she tapped her slender root feet in time with the song on the radio.

"I thought you abhorred all things human?" I said.

"We gave them music and dance. And we always danced to this one."

And that was when I noticed that the song playing was *My Girl*. I hoped it was a coincidence.

"You choose to reside as this..." She waggled her twigs and leaves around me, "but I felt your spirit longing to escape in the dandelion seeds you dispersed. How long will you fester here?"

"This is my home."

"Home?" Her voice raised an octave. "Home is where you can breathe with contentment. Home is where you can feel the heartbeat of the earth. Home is with...m...your family and friends."

"I have friends."

"*His* friends. They'll never understand you."

"*You'll* never understand me." The music on the radio segued to the next song. *By Your Side*. I stared at her. How did she do that? It was against the law, *her* laws, to interfere with human technology.

She came closer. I smelt fresh leaves, sweet petals, scented bark.

I inhaled her oxygen. A drug I had become dependent on. She drew back from my carbon dioxide as though it was tainted with the poison of the boy's kick.

"Why are you here, Mother?"

"It's been a year since we absorbed him into the earth. He sleeps peacefully, yet you lie awake all night."

*He sleeps peacefully.*

That was the irony. Yahya had never been a good sleeper.

It was his midnight gardening that had drawn my attention. He talked to the daffodils and tulips in spring. Sometimes I had opened them up for him, and he had smiled as though the moon was enchanted. Summer twilight helped him to create a canvas of pale pink clematis, multi-coloured begonia and tall gladioli against the dark back fence. He pruned and divided the perennials in autumn and dug the soil over. Neighbouring curtains had twitched, suspecting nefarious nocturnal activity. Especially when he'd sniffed the jasmine and the honeysuckle as though it was the head of his ex-lover.

And often, he'd bring his telescope out of the shed and look into the realms where we had no control.

She brought me out of my reverie.

"You've had your time, bewitching humans and mooching around...
here." She gestured around us with her vines as though I'd made a
poor choice.

"I didn't enchant him." She knew that, of course. I'd seen her peep
through the compost pile three months after I'd arrived home with
Yahya. She'd cast a reversing spell, and when it hadn't worked, she'd
sagged back into the rotting pile of leaves and twigs like a beaten
horse sinking into a boggy pit.

"Most young Jarrican explore the world once they have finished
their studies. You have spent the last nine years in one of the wettest
towns on a densely populated, polluted island."

"I like the rain. It invigorates me. And this whole planet is polluted.
Your laws have seen to that."

"Zya, you've spent so long as a human that you've forgotten what it
is to be Jarrican. *Please*, come home with me."

I'd only ever heard her use the word 'please' once before, and that
was to prevent a war.

"And you've shirked responsibility for long enough."

And there it was. The reason I had chosen the human life.

I placed the mug down on the wooden worktop and pushed it
away from me.

"I'm here, Mother, because it was easy to stay with someone that
looked after me and loved me without question."

"A fool's love...he treated you like a pet...a plant. Fed you, watered
you...you tended to him like a slave!"

My wooden stool fell over as I rose, with my fists clenched by my
side.

"I would like you to leave now, Mother."

She moved towards the open patio doors and looked back.

"Loneliness never settles." She stepped outside, walked onto the
lawn and sank into the ground. The radio started to play. *Reach Out,
I'll Be There.*

For the first time in years, I allowed myself to shift. I let some
carbon dioxide channel through me. My stiffening arms extended
towards the radio, and my twig finger flicked it off before my arm
branch swept it to the floor.

Gliding into Yahya's Garden, I sunk amongst the marigolds. The

dying earth sighed around me.
    I breathed as a Jarrican, devouring the essence of Yahya.

# NEONG CHEE KEIN (ARTHUR)

## *A Walk in the Park*

The walk around the Kota Kemuning MBSA park is two kilometres long, but one would never know when time seemed to creep along as one moved forward.

Albert stopped his car at the designated parking space, turned off the ignition, removed his slippers and replaced them with his old sports shoes. He took his favourite book and climbed out of his battered and scratched 2004 Honda City, which looked so inconspicuous it seemed to fade into the background.

He walked a short distance to the entrance of the park. Beside the entrance, a construction site stood out, with grey building blocks in their initial stages. A private sports complex would be built there soon. The field where residents flew colourful kites in the air was no longer there.

The sight of joggers in colourful attires (mostly 'uncles' and 'aunties', but some looked middle-aged like him) and the grass-covered shore of the man-made lake greeted him at the entrance. A dog lay sleeping on the paved track that marked the start of the two-kilometre loop, and Albert started his walk.

He kept the small book in his blue fanny pack in order to stretch his shoulders (his right hand lifted backwards over his shoulders to reach his left bending upwards at an odd angle, held for fifteen seconds and switched), while trying to maintain a straight path. Several retired-looking men and ladies looked amused as they passed him. He smiled non-committally, half-avoiding their gaze. Around the park, beyond the fence, the houses loomed into view, posh and stately, without gates, like the ones overseas.

He reached the uphill bend at the north-east corner of the park, where the trees were covered with green moss (apparently, indicative of good symbiosis), and a group of retired men were talking. *Perhaps they are not retired, only rich and financially free.* He retrieved the book of short stories from his fanny pack and turned to the second last story. This would be his second time reading it. The fact that he could read it leisurely while walking seemed to cement its greatness. Like Van Gogh, it was years ahead of its time.

Two ladies were talking behind him. By the sound of their growing voices, they were fast approaching him, bonding in English over shared stories and similarities in foreign accents—American and Chinese?

He listened without turning away from his book.

"Oh yes, I am in the process of applying for a visa," said the Chinese lady, heavily accented, but understandable, and sounding quite charming really.

"Yes, I am doing that too," the American voice replied. They passed by him and walked to the front.

*Are they working, I wonder? Or they could be housewives? Or they could be anything.* One didn't need an excuse to come to the public park. Free country. He wondered what the others would be thinking of him, young and in his prime, walking in the park at eight in the morning, a book in hand, sometimes hands folded at the back, this young man who acted old and who did not belong here.

He had reached the last few pages of the short story now. In it, there were descriptions of a pond: 'murky green and infected with moss and dirt.' He could see the similarity in the lake, the moss and dirt hidden away beneath the surface, away from prying eyes, alongside other underwater denizens. Just like the deep, dark ocean. Images of otherworldly creatures seen on YouTube floated to the surface of his mind: skeletal fish with translucent pupils, giant squid with far-reaching tentacles, and a seething mass of slimy, coiling hagfish, burrowing deep into holes and slits of fish carcasses. Though none would be found here in the lake. *Only in the hearts of men. Or perhaps just me.*

Beyond the gazebo was the basketball court, with old people practising tai-chi, their movements graceful and elegant. On the wooden platform of the gazebo lay an old man, sleeping on his side, in his outfit of thin blue shirt hanging loosely and faded black slacks. No slippers. Grey hair, dark skin. He walked past the gazebo, along the other side of the lake, past the gym equipment, some broken, some functioning, yellow under the growing splendour of the sun. Cars were now filling the road to his right, zooming and slowing. He tried hauling himself up onto the monkey bar beyond his reach by way of a small leap and hung there; then moving across one shoulder at a time like an overgrown monkey. He leaped down halfway, his shoulders hurting and feeling the strain. *Yes, in his prime.*

Past the wooden bridge now, bobbing up and down on the planks, the mosque on his right coming into view, magnificent and stately, with a yellow dome and white walls like Taj Mahal in the afternoon. A slender minitower-like structure reached upwards into the sky. Albert's eye was drawn to a similar-looking tree, with a lean trunk that tapered upwards. The view of the tree, with its thinned out faded leaves and whitish pink flowers scattered among them, against the backdrop of the light blue sky looked quite beautiful really. The apparition of a half-moon hung on bravely, still visible against the early light. Framed by rings of clouds, it looked like a lonely island in an ocean of surf, waves and dreams.

He pressed on. Round one complete. The dog was nowhere to be seen. Visitors were heading to their cars now. It was now approaching late morning, when some would want to leave, unwilling to get a tan, while others would head to work, breakfast or go home and potter about. Was he one of them?

Round two. He walked past the start of the path, past the looming houses, past the visitors walking back to their cars. Crows accompanied him, some on the branches above, some on the grassy shore of the lake to his left, hopping about, with twigs in their beaks. Ever industrious, ever vigilant, ever intelligent. Some might consider them a menace, but to Albert, they were quite the role model in more ways than one, embodying traits to look up to, perhaps traits he had to dig deep within to uncover.

Past the uphill stretch now, panting a little along the mostly empty path. His legs still weren't feeling that tired, and ahead, the gazebo awaited. To his right, past the fence, some maids were hanging the laundry by the vast garden.

Spasms of desperate coughing from up ahead broke his reverie.

The old man in the gazebo was sitting up now, his brown skin appearing a shade darker than before. Albert would have walked past him were it not for the wheezing, the alarm on his face, his eyes and mouth like a goldfish on land, and his one hand repeatedly beating his chest. Albert ran up behind him and wrapped his arms around the frantic man, feeling the lonely, frail bones of his ribcage. He felt apprehensive, but at the sound of his insistent coughing, pushed through within, pulled upwards, jerked, repeat. He tried his best to temper his strength for fear of breaking anything, just like one would with a baby. That's what old people are like. Would he be like that one day too? Like a baby?

He lost count how many times he jerked and pulled but after a few moments that felt like forever, an oversized piece of white bread plopped onto the wooden platform. The old man leaned against the pillar, his breaths ragged. Albert stood still for a while, then moved in front to see if he was alright. The old man's breathing seemed calmer now. He eyed Albert gratefully. "Thank you," he started. "Sit. Please."

Albert looked around for a spot, as far away from the wet bread as he possibly could without offending the old man.

"What are you doing here, young man? Don't you need to work?"

*Strange coming from you.* But a legitimate question nonetheless, one he was sure ran through the minds of those he passed by. There was a silence that seemed to stretch into itself, but he eventually answered as truthfully as he could.

"I quit my job, uncle. Now taking a break." There. The standard answer he reserved when asked.

"Oh, what job?"

"Teacher, uncle," Albert said.

"Oh, teacher, ah!" the old man said, with a look of amusement and admiration that seemed all too common, along with that standard reply.

Only these days, they might be thinking 'Better him than me.' Somehow, Albert does not disagree.

"Don't you want to know about me?" the old man asked, with a playful smile on his face, his back still against the pillar, one knee propped up on his chest, his hands resting by his side.

*I know you are homeless. I know you are jobless. Right? We are alike, you and I.* Albert looked down, unable to meet his friendly gaze, wondering what to say. Perhaps, some things are better left unsaid.

"You know, I was a banker last time."

Albert's eyes flicked upwards, his eyebrows arched in surprise.

"I worked in Maybank. Took early VSS retirement package."

"Oh...what happened?" *A lot of money, right?*

The old man looked far away and sighed softly, then turned back to Albert.

"My wife and two children died," he said matter-of-factly, then looked away, blinking a little. His expression was still a bit vacant, as if refusing to let sadness take hold.

A slow pause before Albert said, "I'm sorry" with a look of regret on his face and shared empathy. What if it had happened to him? His wife and two kids?

"After that, I just don't feel like working anymore. What's the point?" The old man paused a while before continuing to explain. "Yes, I will look like this." He gestured at himself and around him, then, "But I sold the car, the house. I just sleep anywhere. I go everywhere. I walk. I take the bus."

Albert listened intently. There was some truth in what the old man had said.

"Like the Lotus Eater? The short story?" Albert ventured.

"Ah, yes! Haha...yes..." The old man grinned, his yellow teeth showing, still intact. "You read it?"

"We read it in Form Four." It had seemed so long ago, yet not too long compared to what it must have been for his comrade in front of him now.

They both regarded each other thoughtfully, for a second or two. Then, the old man said, "Anyway, that's my story."

Albert got up. Seemed like the right time to leave now, after sharing a little about themselves, unlikely acquaintances in an unlikely situation.

"I'm Dhanesh."

"That's a nice name. Thank you for your story, Uncle. I am Albert. Take care. And be careful when eating bread." He pressed his lips in a small smile.

Dhanesh laughed a throaty laugh. His whole face seemed to light up in that moment. "Yes." He nodded his head.

Albert turned to leave and walked past the monkey bar, the half-broken gym equipment, stepped onto the small bridge, the mosque on his right and the calm lake on his left. He walked past the thin flowering tree and other trees which seemed giant in comparison, like massive broccoli in the sky, like the giant multi-coloured lit tree he had once seen in Singapore in one of the tourist attractions. Strange that there could be so many similarities, if one would only look, or had the chance to.

He reached his car, unlocked the door. He started the engine and turned on the aircon and remained standing outside for a while. Then, he drove home, joining the lines of cars that were stuck in traffic now. The road was narrow and two-laned, with trees lining both sides, and would have been lovely were it not for the cars.

When he reached home, he undressed and tossed his sweaty clothes into the laundry basket, before having a long, cold shower. He then changed into comfy pyjamas. He turned on his desktop, his only companion in the now empty house. His wife had left for work, and the kids for school.

He checked his email. No job interviews. He wasn't surprised. Applying for a job where he had no prior experience had seemed like a lost cause. He thought of the skinny old man with the beautiful name Dhanesh.

*The old man is not doing much to live his dream.* Then, *but perhaps he is, by suffering each day, and losing more and more of himself. That takes courage, a different kind of courage, but courage too.*

*What about me? Am I doing much? Am I doing something? Do I have a dream?*

Dhanesh. There was a familiar ring to it. Yes, he had a good friend called Dhanesh in Standard One, who drew and painted beautifully. Albert admired his abilities greatly, though he would never tell him that. Once, Albert had written something down in his diary, a provocative story, and Dhanesh had grabbed it and laughed with a little shock in his eyes. He remembered feeling a form of accomplishment at that.

He typed 'writing workshop' into Google; a list of searches came out. He clicked on them and got redirected to secondary webpages and Facebook sites. Most had been inactive since the Covid pandemic hit three years ago, but one seemed promising. It was a workshop in Penang. He had always secretly wanted to join one, and he recalled thoroughly enjoying the writing workshop that his retired senior assistant had organised when he was still working.

Penang was a four-hour drive away, but it was on a fortnightly basis. It could work. Still, fear of going beyond his comfort zone tugged away at his heart, threatening to sway his mind. *Never mind,* he thought. He would speak to his wife and good friend. Maybe they could tell him what to do.

But for today, he would try something different, instead of looking for jobs, or playing computer games mindlessly. He clicked on his Google Docs and opened a new document. He looked at the screen and paused for a while, images of murky waters, half-moon, flower in the sky replacing the white. And of course, the lotus eater, the brave, brave man who had lost so much and wasn't afraid of losing more. He typed away at the keyboard:

'The walk around the Kota Kemuning MBSA park is two kilometres long, but one would never know when time seemed to creep along as one moved forward.'

Not perfect really, but as good a start as any.

# MARY ONIONS

## *Grounded*

There's a steep bit along Blind Lane where you can feel like you're flying. It makes me think of that children's poem we read in school about riding downhill on a bike.

*Swifter and yet more swift,*
*Till the heart with a mighty lift*
*Makes the lungs laugh*

I always like the idea of the 'lungs laughing'. It seems so complete somehow. So joyous. And it's hard not to laugh when you're out cycling on a spring morning, the whitethorn dusting the hedges, the birds singing, and the daffodils nodding in the breeze doing the whole Wordsworth thing.

I'm going full throttle now. Glancing down at my odometer I see I'm touching 55. A bubble of hysteria rises in my throat. Then, out of the corner of my eye, I see it. The pothole. I swerve to avoid it and cycle on, unscathed. Ha! Can't get me! I am invincible! I raise my hands; the Tour de France winner acknowledging applause as she crosses the line. And at that moment a mob of neon yellow lycra-clad men appear around the bend hurtling towards me. There is no way out. My bike wobbles beneath me, tipping me headlong into the hedge. I don't see the bramble. I don't see anything. The pain is so intense I can't open my eyes. I am aware of a shocked silence as the lycra lads must have abandoned their bikes and gathered around me. "You all right love?"

No. I am not all right. I awake to darkness. To pain. Everything hurts. My mouth is dry, my head is throbbing and my leg, for some reason, seems to be up in the air. I can't see. Why is it so dark? I reach up to my eyes and feel a bandage.

"Uh, uh. Don't touch."

Someone is next to me, swatting my hand away from the bandage.

"That needs to stay there until the morning. Doctor's orders."

The voice is friendly, but firm, with a Caribbean lilt. It sounds like sunshine.

"What…" I try to speak but my tongue is stuck to the roof of my mouth.

"Here, drink this."

Ms Sunshine puts my hands around a plastic cup. She guides my fingers to a straw protruding from the top and helps me raise it to my lips. I gulp down some water. It's warm and stale, but delicious.

"Thank you," I manage.

"Good to see you awake at last. The rest of the ward will be happy too. You were snoring up a storm there, girl."

"Where…" I start but she's ahead of me.

"St. Olaf's, darling. Trauma."

"But…"

"You had a bike accident. Broke your leg and scratched your eyes,"

"Am I…"

"Blind? Probably not. You'll know when these come off." She taps my bandages lightly.

Probably not? What does that mean? Does that mean possibly yes? I might be blind? This can't be happening to me. I need to see. I try to sit up but realise I can't. My leg is in traction. Blind and immobile. This is ridiculous.

"Excuse me," I shout. Nothing. "Hello? Is there anyone there?"

Footsteps. Then, "Hey girl, you shush. You wanna wake everyone up again? First the snoring, then the shouting. It's the middle of night."

"How am I supposed to know that? I can't see a thing."

"True. But you can hear, can't you? Ain't no other noises here 'cept you shouting your mouth off."

I sense that she is about to walk away.

"Wait—what about my leg?"

"You smashed your tibia. Nasty. But it's gonna be fine. Surgery tomorrow. You'll be up and running again in about six months." Her sneakers squeak as she walks off.

Six months! I can't be stuck like this for six months! I realise I have no idea how long I've been here. What day is it? What about Tokyo?

I lie fretting as the hours crawl by. I'm stuck, imprisoned in this ridiculous position, like one of those old cartoons. It's not just the discomfort that paralyses me, though. It's the fear of blindness that keeps my mind racing. I try to blink, to see through the bandages, but they're wound round thick and tight. I can't be blind. I just can't. I try to imagine what life would be like. Never again to see the sky filled with oranges and yellows as we fly east, or the tip of Mt. Fuji poking up through the clouds, or the immeasurably vast frozen plains of Siberia. Flying is my life. I simply can't imagine what I'd do instead. And what will they be thinking at work when I don't turn up? My first flight as Captain. The youngest captain ever. The youngest female captain ever. I can just imagine the jokey blokey comments being made.

And there's something else niggling away at the back of my mind. I can't seem to reach it. My thoughts go round and round.

It's a long night.

Morning brings the doctor and good news.

"Well, your cornea seems to be healing nicely so we can get rid of the bandages, but better to wear dark glasses for a while."

The relief is so great I burst into tears. He sighs. He's seen it all. He tries to sound upbeat.

"I'm afraid that leg's a bit of a mess, though. Never mind. We'll have you in theatre this morning and put it right. You'll soon be up and about again."

I'm not worried about the leg. Broken legs heal, don't they? I can see. I can still fly. That's all that matters. But I need to phone work. Explain. Where is my phone? Don't tell me it's still in the hedge?

Ms Sunshine finds it in my jacket pocket. The glass is smashed but it still works. Thank God.

There are a ton of missed calls and messages. Mostly from Tish. Tish! Oh God! That's what I was trying to remember. My stomach twists. She'll be furious. I absolutely promised I'd be there.

"Mel, where the hell are you? The table's booked for seven. We'll have to meet you there."

"Mel? You promised. You can't just buy your way out of this with an expensive gift. Again."

"Stuff you, Mel."

I'm aware of Ms Sunshine standing by, needle in hand, listening.

"Uh, oh. Someone's not happy with you."

"My sister," I explain.

"Aren't you gonna phone her back?"

"In a minute. I've got to contact work first."

"Well don't take too long. They want you in surgery in ten minutes."

Jack at work manages to be sympathetic and accusatory at the same time. They had to juggle the schedule and draft in some newbie who'd never done long haul before he tells me, somehow implying that that was all my fault.

I feel guilty, then angry. I've never been so much as ten minutes late. I'm the one they call at short notice. They assume it's easy for me. No husband or kids waiting at home complaining that I'm never there. I've just got Tish. Now that Mum's gone. Why is it OK to take time off for your husband or your kids but not for your mother or your sister? Don't they count?

Really though? An inner voice questions me. Did you really want to spend time looking after Mum? Or were you only too glad to take all those long-distance flights? I tell my inner voice to shut up.

When I wake up from surgery, sick and groggy, Tish is sitting by my bed.

"OK, you're forgiven," she says. "I don't believe even you would have arranged for this just to get out of a birthday dinner."

She offers me her spare room, 'just till you're back on your feet', but I insist I'll be OK. Do I imagine the look of relief on her face?

She promises to pop by from time to time, to check I'm OK. Then she smiles and grabs my hand.

"You know, this might be good for you. A bit of enforced R and R. You've hardly stopped this past year."

She stays and chats for a bit but my eyes keep closing. When I wake up, she's gone.

So perhaps I was a bit over ambitious. Always my problem, according to Mum. Getting around with a broken leg is not easy. I stand in the hallway looking at the stairs. Not a chance of getting up those for a while.

I'm proud of my little house. The previous owner was about a hundred years old and the flowery wallpaper and swirly carpet must have been almost the same age. I watched all the DIY programmes on TV, looked at colour schemes and paints and gave it a complete makeover. It meant spending all my days off scraping and peeling and painting and varnishing but the end result was worth it. My best decision, I realise, was to turn the dining room into a study with a sofa bed.

I get as far as this and collapse on the bed. Why did no one tell me crutches were so difficult? I must have been more tired than I realised because when I wake up the afternoon sun is casting a warm glow on the photo of Mum on the desk.

I heave myself off the bed, leaning heavily on the crutches and hobble along to the kitchen, where I put the kettle on and realise I can't reach the tea bags on the top shelf. And of course, there's no milk anyway. The fridge holds a pack of butter, a bottle of wine and some rather mouldy cheese. I'm supposed to be in Tokyo this week, so why I've let supplies run low.

I've opened the wine and scraped the mould off the cheese when I hear someone at the front door.

"Hope you don't mind me letting myself in. You did give me a key, remember."

Tish, bless her, has brought bread and milk and fruit and a whole bunch of ready meals. She bustles round the kitchen, making sure that everything I need is in reach. Then she goes upstairs and brings down sheets, towels and a pile of clothes. She puts fresh sheets on the bed.

I watch her in admiration. "You're really good at this, aren't you?"

"I've had lots of practice."

Uh, oh, I think, here it comes. The 'I did everything for Mum and you did nothing' complaint. Get over it, I think. That was three years ago.

But she just smiles and says, "There, I think that's everything. I'd better dash."

I find I don't want her to go.

"Can't you stay for a glass of wine?" I wave the wine bottle, in what

I hope is a tempting way, but my voice sounds sad, pathetic. She looks at me in surprise. Pretends not to notice the tears welling up in my eyes.

"Just a quick one, then. And make it a small one. I've got to pick Jenny up from training."

"She still set on becoming the next Victoria Pendleton?"

"Oh yes. Totally focused. Nothing else matters!"

"Well, tell her not to break her leg."

I try to remember the last time I just sat and had a drink with Tish. It must have been Christmas. Well the day after Boxing Day. Nobody else wants to work during the holiday. I'd just flown in from Bali, and England had never seemed colder, wetter or darker. I was jet-lagged and she and Jenny were in that post Christmas slump. I'd bought Jenny some Hello Kitty merchandise from the Duty Free and realised too late it was far too young for her. She's a nice kid and tried to sound enthusiastic but the visit wasn't a resounding success. It's been a bit awkward between us ever since.

We chat for a while and I tell her that I've been signed off work for at least three months. I am dreading it.

"You never know. You might find you enjoy it." She tries to sound reassuring before she dashes off.

The days crawl by. I watch far too much daytime television full of adverts for mobility scooters and chairs that rise and fall at the push of a button. I'm almost tempted to buy one of these as getting up from the sofa involves a delicate balance of pushing down on the crutches and pulling myself up and grunting. Lots of grunting. Jenny phones every couple of days. It's good to hear her. Not that I've got anything much to tell her.

Gradually I get used to hobbling around. I even manage to have a shower, taping a huge plastic bag to my leg. I get quite adept in the kitchen, juggling crutches and kettles and pans. I even start to cook properly. The supermarket delivery service is proving a godsend.

But the days are long. I brood and look out of the window, jealous at all the people hurrying by. They don't need to think about the simple act of walking. They just take it for granted. I move to the back of the house and look out at the garden. A cluster of little birds are clinging on to a wire feeder on the neighbour's beech tree.

I watch the old man next door. He's dug over the raised beds and now he's preparing little pots of seedlings from the greenhouse to plant outdoors. He does this tenderly, but with precision. Using a ruler to check the exact distances between each hole he prepares for them. Then he tucks them in gently and takes up the watering can, sprinkling them with water. I can't hear anything but it looks as though he's talking to the plants.

He sees me at the door and gives a wave. I duck inside. I don't do old people. They're too needy.

It's soothing, though, watching someone else work. Real, physical work as Tish would say. She's a plumber. Spends her time unblocking people's toilets and healing dripping taps. She's the only woman in a man's world and very popular with the old ladies.

"I don't understand how you can do that," I said to her once.

"It works well with Jenny and her competitions. I can choose my hours. Besides, I like helping people.".

"Well, I help people too. I help them get where they want to go."

"Yea and fill the air with filth. Your carbon footprint must be off the scale. Didn't the pandemic teach you anything?"

Only that I hated being grounded.

The weather's getting warmer. I hobble out to the garden and sit in the sun, watching the little birds. They've made a nest in an old wooden bird box nailed to the tree. I wonder how long it takes for chicks to hatch. I should google it, but the computer's in the study and I can't be bothered to move. I look up at the sky. Tiny silver bullets pass overhead, leaving broad contrails in their wake that dissolve as I watch them. I feel so jealous. I want to be back up there, going somewhere. Anywhere other than here.

Out of the corner of my eye I see movement. A black cat slithers under the fence and approaches the tree. She crouches under the bird box, waiting. A flutter of wings from above and she rises, ready to pounce.

"Don't you dare!" I yell. The cat takes no notice, intent on its prey. I jump up out of my deckchair, trying to throw my crutch at it. And fall flat on my face.

The man next door sticks his head over the fence.

"Everything all right over there?"

I'm lying on the ground, what does he think?

"Is that your cat?" I shout

"No, it's from number 43, bloody nuisance. Do you need a hand?"

I start to say I'm fine, but I'm not. I'm flailing around like a beached whale.

"I'll come round."

A few minutes later he's next to me, reaching out an arm, dragging me to my feet and holding out my crutches. He's strong for an old man.

"Thank you." I say and promptly burst into tears.

"Hey, hey. It's nothing to cry about." He sounds embarrassed, concerned. "Look just sit down and I'll get you a cup of tea."

He comes back with two mugs and a packet of chocolate biscuits.

It's the biscuits that get me. Chocolate Hobnobs. My favourite. Mum's favourite. I burst into tears again.

He looks at me helplessly. "It's tough, isn't it, being in plaster? But it'll pass."

"I know, I know," I sob. "But I hate not being able to get around. I should be on my way to Tokyo right now. Flying one of those—I point to a passing plane high in the sky. Instead, I'm stuck here looking at wrens or whatever they are being attacked by a lousy cat."

"They're swifts, actually. Fastest birds around. Sixty-nine miles per hour. Every year they fly a total of 3,400 miles. Isn't that amazing?"

"It's 5,956 miles to Tokyo. Thirteen hours and five minutes at an average speed of 500 mph," I retort.

"Yes, but you must admit, you have help. These birds don't have jet engines. They just fly. They do everything on the wing, eat, sleep and even mate."

"Sounds exhausting. And rather difficult."

He gives a short bark of a laugh. "Yes, talk about the mile high club!" He pauses and asks with a twinkle, "Is that a real thing?"

Yuk! Is he coming on to me? He must be at least 70. A 70-year-old twitcher, just what I need.

He notes my expression. "Sorry, bad taste. I'd better be off."

He picks up the mugs, leaves me the biscuits and disappears.

Oh dear. I obviously misread that situation. He seems a nice guy. He was just being friendly. When did I become Miss Prude?

I talk to Tish about him next time she calls. She laughs.

"Oh Mel, you were always prudish. Looking offended when the girls talked about sex or boys or whatever. My mates were always a bit intimidated by you to be honest."

I wasn't offended. I just didn't know how to respond. I never realised I intimidated people.

I've never been very good at small talk. Or making friends for that matter. I was always too shy at school and had to pretend I didn't care that I wasn't part of the cool crowd. While Tish and her gang of friends were giggling and gossiping and sneaking a smoke behind the bike sheds, I'd be in the library, hiding away, studying for my exams. I think that's when I decided to be a pilot. What a way to escape. To fly away from it all.

I feel bad about Next Door Man. He was only trying to help. I make sure I get some chocolate biscuits in my delivery and next time I see him in the garden I invite him over.

He seems surprised, but pleased and insists on helping carry out the mugs and plates. His name is Brian and he's not an expert on birds, he just likes swifts and googled them. He asks about my job and I tell him about the enduring thrill of feeling the huge plane lift off from the ground and climb. I tell him of the views from the cockpit of snow-capped mountain ranges, shimmering azure oceans, the vast sprawl of the Tokyo metropolis. The whole world spread out at your feet.

"Tokyo's fascinating, isn't it?" he says. "That Shibuya Crossing! The whole world seems to be on the move there. And such great food! I bet you and the crew have a great time, exploring all the bars and restaurants. How's your karaoke?"

I don't tell him that while the rest of the crew head out on the town, I just go to my hotel room and read. I feel awkward. There's a sort of hierarchy between the pilots and the flight attendants, so they never feel comfortable with me. And the other pilots are always male and either flirty or patronising. I mumble something about liking to do things on my own.

"Yea, I get that. Like cycling. I prefer cycling on my own to riding with a group."

I think of the neon clad men in my crash and bemoan the loss of my bike. We talk about possible replacements. He's quite knowledgeable, or is he just enjoying a bit of mansplaining?

"Don't be so ready to criticise," says Tish, later. "He sounds perfectly nice. A decent bloke."

The next day he invites me over for dinner. He's thinking he might get some Japanese food, to make up for me missing out on Tokyo.

"Isn't that thoughtful of him," says Tish on the phone. "What are you going to wear?"

"It's not a date. He's old enough to be our father."

"You're not getting any younger yourself."

I decide to dress up anyway. I've worn nothing but sweat pants and tee shirts since the accident. This is quite an effort as my one good dress is upstairs. I sit on the bottom step and edge myself up backwards one step at a time. I find my one good dress and fling it over the banister, then bump back down to retrieve it. I even put on some make-up. I'm glad I did. When he comes to the door, I see he's made a bit of an effort too. He's wearing smart chinos and a collared shirt, open at the neck.

We sip the sake I've brought and eat plump pink salmon sashimi, glossy green edamame and crispy prawn tempura, all set out on little blue and white pottery plates.

"Where did you get all these lovely dishes?"

"There's a great little shop in Shimo-Kitazawa I found last time I was in Tokyo. Have you ever been there?"

I'm too embarrassed to say that all I really know of Tokyo is from the air, looking down on the city and suburbs that spread for miles from the ocean to Mount Fuji. I've always been too shy or too scared to venture out on my own.

I change the subject. Ask him about his garden. The French doors are open and I can see it clearly for the first time. It is extraordinary. Not the neat borders I expected but a riot of different plants. There are tulips and daffodils of course, but there's a little rock garden with alpine flowers, a delicate Japanese maple and in the corner a palm tree.

"Do you like it? Most people think it's a total mess, but it suits me." He points out the different plants, telling me how they remind him of places he's been.

Later I excuse myself to go to the loo. His house is the reverse of mine, with the same little study in the front. I can't resist pushing open the door and having a peep. Along one wall is a large cabinet, full of trophies and medals. On another are two large frames, one with a yellow jersey and one with a pink one. As quietly as possible, I manoeuvre myself into the room for a closer look.

I'm bending down to examine one of the trophies when he appears in the doorway.

"Ah, I see you've found my glory room."

I stumble against the cabinet. He grabs me before I fall, retrieves my crutches.

"You won the Tour de France!" It comes out almost as an accusation.

"Just the first stage, on the first day."

"That's incredible. Wait till I tell Jenny!" I explain that my niece is determined to be a champion cyclist. I ask him, tentatively, if she could meet him.

Three days later I find myself hosting a dinner party for the three of them. The chicken is a bit dry and the potatoes are soggy but no one notices the food.

Jenny bombards Brian with questions; for me and Tish they might as well be speaking a foreign language as they discuss pacelines and pelotons, leadouts and jumps.

Brian takes pity on us and talks more generally of the differences between road racing and track cycling, between the Tour de France, Le Giro and La Vuelta. He tells us about the adrenalin rush, the sheer thrill of crossing the line seconds ahead of his rivals.

"Why did you stop?" asks Jenny.

"I broke my leg, love. Just like Mel here. And that gave me time to think. At first I didn't know what to do with myself. I'd spent years focusing on chasing my dream. I'd train every day. And I mean every single day. My family got fed up with it. I'm not surprised. I was either training or competing. I missed birthdays, anniversaries, even the birth of my son. In the end it was just too much for them. I don't blame them. It's a selfish business."

He pauses and takes a gulp of his wine. He looks directly at Jenny.

"People tell you to follow your dreams, but they never tell you about the cost."

"But you got to do all those tours," protests Jenny. "You went all over the world."

"Yes, but I didn't really see anything. We'd cycle 200 miles through the most glorious scenery and all I'd see were the bottoms of the blokes in front of me bobbing up and down in their saddles. The Pyrenees, the Japanese Alps, they were literally just more mountains to climb. And after all that someone would beat you by tenths of a second. Ridiculous.

"So I decided that I actually wanted to see some of the places I'd cycled through. I'd never had time to stop and stare, as they say. I went back and cycled them slowly. I stopped for cold beers in tiny villages that I hadn't even noticed as I'd dashed past them. I lay on my back in fields of sunflowers. I paused to admire the view from each hairpin bend. It was so peaceful. So different from the races when all you see is the road in front of you, the wheels of the peloton and the occasional idiot jumping out from the crowd to take a picture. You have to focus on the road ahead, but you miss so much along the way."

Another gulp of wine, then.

"You know, close up, the world is a beautiful place."

I'm not sure, but I think this is directed at me.

Not long after that, I have the plaster removed. It's a strange feeling, like my leg is floating on air. And I'm free. Free to go to the hospital every day for physio, free to watch Jenny's training sessions. Free to meet Tish for coffee.

"Thanks for having us over," she tells me. "Jenny has been buzzing ever since. She's struck up quite a friendship with Brian. She can discuss all the technical stuff with him. He's been along to watch her train. He's a really nice guy."

I raise an eyebrow. "Indeed?"

She blushes, "He's not that old, you know".

She looks younger, happier, less stressed as she carries on, "I think he had a real impact on her, you know. All that about losing his family. Jenny has agreed to at least one rest day a week, but only on condition that we do something together. She doesn't want to lose me she says."

"Neither do I," I find myself saying. "It's been good, seeing more of you."

She smiles, surprised. "It's been nice having you around, Mel."

And that's it. That's enough. We don't really do emotional scenes, but we know that we're back on track.

A few weeks later I'm back to work. Brian has promised to water the strawberries and beans I've planted while I'm away and Tish is going to fill the fridge for when I get back.

In my cabin baggage I have the details of the pottery shop in Shimo-Kitazawa and the address for 'the best ramen restaurant in the world', according to Brian. He's right. It's daft to only see these places from afar. Close up, the world can be a beautiful place.

I'm tempted to throw the crutches away, but think better of it. You never know when life will stop you in your tracks again.

---

# *Pilgrimage*

Michael scans the towering red rocks ahead of him. He's Butch Cassidy, keeping a wary watch for bounty hunters. He thinks he sees a white hat disappearing behind a distant outcrop. "Who is that guy?" he mutters. He considers crouching beneath a ledge, then quickens his pace as he spies a cave up ahead. The trail lies before him, dry and dusty. He wonders if it ever rains here; this wild expanse of brown, orange and red, barren save for patches of tired, scrubby bushes. The cave, when he reaches it, looks cool and dark. A fine place to shelter from the bounty hunters and the heat. But of course, he can't go in. He checks his watch. Another ten minutes to go. He can make it. He keeps walking.

The sound of a key in the lock.

"It's only me!" Julie calls, kicking the front door shut behind her. Laden with Sainsbury's bags, she staggers down the hallway to the kitchen, pausing in the doorway.

"Where is it today, Dad?"

"Shh, they'll hear you."

She comes into the room, looks at the screen.

"Ah, the Cassidy Trail. OK Butch, you've got this. Coffee in five, if you make it out of there alive."

Michael smiles, turns the dial, slowing gradually to a stop. The screen fades to black. He takes his towel, wipes his face and follows her into the kitchen.

Julie is filling the fridge with groceries. Yoghurt, lettuce, carrots and cabbage.

"More rabbit food?"

"You've got to eat more healthily, Dad. You can't live on ready meals."

"Bet Butch Cassidy didn't eat yoghurt."

"What do you want? Pork and beans round the campfire? You should try somewhere else. Like the Dolomites or Lake Garda. Get some decent pasta."

"Yea, maybe some pizza. Did you get…"

"Yes. It's in the freezer."

"Thanks love. Don't know what I'd do without you."

Julie puts some apples in the fruit bowl and turns to him.

"We were wondering if you wanted to come over on Sunday. Freya's birthday. I'm doing a roast, making a cake."

"I'm not sure."

"You haven't seen her for ages."

"She came round just last week. I helped her with her Maths."

"She wants to show off her new bedroom."

They lock eyes. It's a challenge. They both know that that would entail him actually leaving the house. Michael is the first to look away.

"I'll think about it," he promises, as he has done so many times before.

When she's gone, he feels ashamed. He really should try, for her sake. And for Freya's. He stands by the kitchen door, looking out on the garden. The lawn, once his pride and joy, looks unkempt. Patches of moss vie with the grass and the daisies. He should mow it. It wouldn't take long. It could be a first step. First the garden, then the street, then who knows? He might even make it to Julie's on Sunday.

What did that counsellor say? Baby steps.

No time like the present, he tells himself. He sits on the stool, pulls on his boots, then hesitates.

Deep breaths.

One step at a time.

He gets as far as the shed. The rusty bolt squeals as he opens it. He drags the lawnmower out.

He can do this.

As he starts to push the mower over the grass something catches his eye. A large black shape hurtles from the sky. He can see it, twisting and turning. He sees a face, its mouth open in a scream he can't hear.

Everything goes black.

When he comes to, he is still clinging to the lawnmower, trembling. He stays there for a long time, waiting for the shakes to subside.

Later he rationalises. It was only a crow. Or a blackbird. Why wouldn't you expect to see a bird in your garden? He'll try again tomorrow. Or the next day.

In the meantime, he goes back to his trails. Julie was right. He should try some new ones. Less threatening ones. Perhaps it was the red bleakness of the Cassidy Trail that had spooked him even before the crow. He should try somewhere calmer, greener.

It was Freya who'd told him about the app, though it was Julie who'd got him the treadmill.

For the first few weeks after the incident, he'd done nothing. He'd been given time off work, of course. Standard procedure in cases like his. They'd even arranged for him to have counselling, but he found that frustrating. The counsellor kept wanting him to talk about his childhood. As if that had anything to do with it. He was on the point of giving up, jacking it all in, but his boss pointed out that he needed the medical certificate to be officially signed off.

"You've only got a few more months till retirement, Mike. You'd be daft to lose your full pension."

So, he stuck it out for a while longer. He pretended to Julie that it was helping, but he found that after each session the nightmares were even worse. And he had incidents during the day. Panic attacks, Julie called them. He'd see the black bundle hurtling towards him and he'd black out. When he came to, he'd find himself shaking uncontrollably, gasping for breath. He'd try to remember the counsellor's advice.

"Stand still. Close your eyes. Breathe deep."

Sometimes it worked.

Julie nagged him to get out of the house, telling him he would feel better in the fresh air.

He tried. He really did. But he would get as far as the postbox at the end of the Close and stop. He'd stand there, paralysed with indecision. To turn right led to the bridge over the tracks and he obviously couldn't go there. So, he'd turn left and walk round the Close, back to his own front door. Sometimes he did the same circle half a dozen times. He never could take the right turn. His neighbours were concerned. They spoke to Julie; said they were worried about him. So he stopped going out altogether. He didn't need to. Julie did his food shopping and anything else he ordered online.

Julie tried another tack.

"If you won't walk outside, we'll have to think of an alternative. You need exercise, Dad. Look at you. You used to be really fit. Freya was saying that you're like an old man now. You never used to be."

She was right. He had been proud of his fitness. He used to walk for miles along the coastal path or up over the Downs. Now his face in the mirror was grey, his eyes dull. His belly was in free fall over his belt, which he'd had to loosen to the farthest notch. He got breathless going upstairs and he'd started to make a grunting noise when he got up from the sofa.

Something had to be done.

Hence the treadmill.

He liked the mindless monotony of it. Putting one foot in front of the other, going nowhere slowly. It was safe here in the living room. He'd watch the step counter tick over, giving him a sense of making progress. He listened to music as he walked, making playlists to amuse himself. *Walking on the Wild Side* with Lou Reed, *On the Road Again* with Willie Nelson and *Walking the Line* with Johnny Cash. It was far more therapeutic than the counselling sessions.

His clothes started to fit more comfortably. He stood up straighter. He stopped grunting.

But the nights were still bad. The same dream over and over again. The black bundle falling towards him. His anger that someone would throw a bag of rubbish on the tracks. Then the realisation. The flailing arms, the billowing black dress, the white face, the mouth a perfect O. And every night it ended the same. The frantic rush to apply the brakes, knowing that it was already far too late. The screeching halt. The deathly silence. He'd lie there in the darkness wondering what could have led her to such a desperate act. Was it a spur of the moment decision? Because she definitely jumped. She couldn't have fallen. The wall on the bridge was far too high for such an accident. And that expression on her face. What did it mean? It wasn't shock or fear. It nagged away at him. Why had she done it?

And what about those she left behind? He knew she had a mother. They said the body had to be identified by dental records. How could a mother cope with that? He thought of Julie and Freya and his insides turned to water. He'd wanted to write to her, the mother, but when it came to it, he couldn't think of anything to say, except, "I'm sorry."

During the day he walked, clocking up the miles. In a month he'd walked 500 miles. Freya played him The Proclaimers to celebrate. Then she showed him the app that changed it all.

"You can go anywhere you want, Grandad. The Inca Trail, the Alps, Kathmandu, Rio de Janeiro. You just click on here and off you go."

To begin with, he'd balance the iPad on the treadmill and squint at the path ahead. Then Freya showed him how to hook it up to his large flat screen TV. It was a revelation. The whole world opened up before him. He could lose himself among the rice terraces of Bali, or the mountain monasteries of Lhasa, or by the thundering waters at Niagara. And as he walked, his imagination ran wild. He became an archaeologist investigating neolithic sites in the Orkneys, or a busy commuter rushing through the streets of Tokyo, or a cowboy in the Wild West. And as he did so, the dark world of his nightmares started to recede.

But not entirely disappear.

And he still can't leave the house. He doesn't make it to Julie's for dinner on Sunday. Instead, they bring the cake to him and they sit around the kitchen table as Freya shares her plans for her gap year. He's prepared to discuss the relative merits of Thailand and Cambodia; he's been to both on the treadmill. But Freya surprises him. Tells him that she's thinking of walking the Camino de Santiago. It's a pilgrimage, apparently.

"Have you gone and got religion, love?" he asks, surprised.

She tells him her friend's mother has cancer and they want to raise money for Cancer Research.

"Like a sponsored walk?"

"Yea, that sort of thing."

"Sounds like a right good idea. I'll sponsor you. Course I will."

"Thank you. But..." She pauses, looking to her mother for help.

"Go on, ask him," says Julie.

"I was thinking that we could, like, do it together."

She laughs at the expression on his face.

"Not really, obvs, but you could do it virtually. On the treadmill. I bet there's an app for it. It might, I dunno, give you, like, a purpose to all that walking you do."

"It'd be more useful than playing cowboys," Julie points out.

He's touched that his granddaughter wants to share the experience, but he's bothered by the implication. Is that what they thought? That his walking just some silly game? He's still brooding a bit as they say goodbye. Julie points to a stack of post piled up on the hall table.

"You really should look at those, Dad. They might be important."

He promises to open them later. He takes the pile into the living room and sits at the computer. The idea that he's wasting his time rankles. Is there any difference between playing cowboys and playing pilgrims? It helped him, but was he being selfish? Maybe he could help the girls raise some money, show them he can do something useful. Julie would like that. He starts to research the Camino de Santiago.

Michael doesn't believe in fate. There's no divine or supernatural power directing us, he'd say. There's good luck and bad luck and coincidence. It wasn't fate that made the girl jump in front of his train. It was coincidence she chose that bridge and bad luck that he happened to be driving towards it. End of.

But just occasionally a coincidence comes along that stops you in your tracks.

He is about to go to bed, when he sees the pile of mail. He flicks through it, stopping at a thick official looking envelope from the office. He opens it, thinking it is about his pension. "'Bout time," he mutters.

But it isn't that at all. Inside is a handwritten letter. He scans it quickly, then backs down onto the sofa. He fumbles for his glasses and reads more carefully.

*Dear Michael*

*We don't know each other, but you wrote me a note once and I never replied.*

*It was my daughter who jumped in front of your train.*

*There I've said it. It's taken me a long time to admit that she jumped. I used to tell everyone she fell, but we both know that's not true, don't we?*

His heart is thumping as he forces himself to read on. She's not writing to blame him, she says. She's writing because she's recently done a pilgrimage, the Camino de Santiago. He gives a little laugh.

How's that for coincidence, he thinks.

*I'm not religious or anything. I stopped believing in God when Lily died. What sort of God would let that happen? But I discovered everybody has their own Camino; some are doing it for spiritual enlightenment, some to keep fit or defy old age, and some are just so full of grief and guilt that they don't know what else to do except try to put one foot in front of the other and keep on going.*

*I knew which category I fell into.*

It's quite a long letter. She tells him about her anger as she stomped her way up the Roncesvalles Pass at the beginning of the walk, railing at the weather, her blistered feet, the other pilgrims, but mostly at Lily.

*Why had she done such a thing? How could she have done that to me?* There's quite a lot of description of the walk, the crowded dormitories smelling of damp socks, the tiny town and villages, the vineyards. He makes a mental note to look up the places she mentions. It's interesting, but he's not sure why she'll telling him all this.

Until the end.

*So why am I writing to you?*

*Because your note said, 'I'm sorry'. I think you may be feeling guilty and guilt is so corrosive, isn't it? Believe me, I know. I felt so much guilt after Lily died. It haunted me. Paralysed me. But you have a lot of time to think on the Camino. You fall into a rhythm. Your feet march on to your destination and your mind is free to roam. And over the miles I came to realise it wasn't about me. It was never about me. We all have our own paths to take and our own decisions to make. Lily's ended far too early, but that was the path she chose. I like to think that, in the end, she found peace. She had made her decision. I hope she found relief in that.*

The page blurs before his eyes. He takes out a handkerchief and blows his nose noisily. It's the word 'relief' that gets him. That's the expression on the face he sees every night in his dreams. Had Lily let go? Had she found relief?

*I will always be heartbroken that she made that choice, but I no longer feel so guilty. I've laid that particular burden down.*

*I hope that you are able to do that too.*

*Grace*

He puts the letter down gently on the sofa. How was it that this letter arrived today of all days? And how does this woman, Grace, understand him so well?

That night he dreams again. As usual the body falls towards him, twisting and twirling, but tonight it seems to slow down. Michael can see her face clearly. Yes, she knows exactly what she's doing. She looks relieved. She's chosen her path. He turns over and sleeps soundly for the first time in a very long time.

In the morning he investigates the Camino, looking up all the places Grace mentioned in her letter. He prints out an itinerary, puts the sheets of paper into a plastic folder.

He doesn't know if he will be able to do the walk in reality or virtually, but he has to start somewhere. He finds his jacket and shoes and opens the front door. Takes a deep breath.

One step at a time, he tells himself.

Then he picks up the folder and walks down the Close. At the corner he turns right.

KATIE RIZZO

_____

## *Endless Horizon*

Kristen Neuschafer's white-toothed smile and suntanned face radiates out from the front page of the Washington Post. Sonya traces Kristen's smile with her pointer finger while she eats breakfast. Her husband sits across from her in their designer kitchen. The headline *Winner of the Ultimate Around the World Sailing Race* is centered above Kristen's half-page headshot.

Sonya skims the article as she picks the psoriasis on her hairline. Sailors in this competition were not allowed to use GPS, or any technology that uses a plug. They also could not go ashore as they navigated around the world. Kristen spent the last eight months fully alive as her rosy glow attests. She was surprised she won; Kristen was so invested in the process that the outcome seemed unimportant. She goes so far as to say, "Nine out of every ten days on the water were amazing." When asked about her lowest point during the race she recalls, "The boat was still, the water was a dead calm. I was pretty sure I'd lost the competition in the windless doldrums. I was frustrated by the lack of movement. You can't just make the wind pick up! So, I did the only thing I could think to do: I dove into the water and swam to the endless horizon. Once I got tired I looked back. I almost couldn't see my ship." The article doesn't note if she wore a life vest during this epic swim.

Sonya finishes her buttered toast and stares out at their neon green lawn. The landscapers were just here so the grass still has the hatch marks from the mower.

"Pete! Did you see this crazy woman?" Sonya slides the article over.

Pete gulps down his coffee and gives the article a cursory glance.

"Yeah, boy. That's something."

Pete gets up and pulls his tie out. It was tucked under the third button of his white dress shirt. He presses the blue paisley design down flat. "I've got a full day in court. You need anything with the kids?" He kisses her head and he heads to the kitchen.

Sonya rolls her eyes but it's lost on Pete. He's already dumping his dishes into the sink. The clatter is enough to make her turn.

Just last week there was an article on how women do at least two more hours of housework a day than men. They'd both read it and laughed; Pete said it was because women cared how the house looked.

In Alanon, she'd learned to put her head down and do the work, even if it wasn't fair. They told the story of the nagging woman who always made coffee for meetings. She complained to someone and he asked her if she minded making the coffee. She responded that she actually liked the act of putting grinds in and adding water, but disliked that no one else helped. He said it sounded like the problem wasn't with the coffee but with her attitude. The moral of the story: make the coffee and keep your mouth shut.

It wasn't that she spent so much more time on housework than Pete that bothered Sonya. It was the emotional labor that wore her down: the planning, lists, and organizing. Each family member's happiness and success somehow got tied to Sonya. Pete laughed when she talked about emotional labor. He said if you drop a ball, I'll pick it up, and if I don't it must not have been that important.

"Do you think that woman, Kristen, will be able to settle down now, compromise with her day and live a normal life? I mean how will anything compare to so many months at sea?"

Pete laughs, "Only you'd ask about her return home."

"What do you mean by that?"

"Well, the rest of us are wondering how she paid for an eight-month vacation on a yacht. You're worried she's gonna have trouble acclimating to real life."

Pete grabs his black Patagonia backpack and shoves his laptop inside.

She watches as he pulls the straps over his well-defined arms and evaporates to the carport. The kids hadn't changed his body as much as they did hers. Sonya grabs her belly and gives it a little shake. No matter how hard she tries, those ten pounds don't go anywhere.

The kids' feet pound down the stairs. Their normal voices register at the level of a muscle car without its muffler. Ever since the boys entered puberty, they take up the whole room with their bodies, noises, smells and opinions. Miles juggles a soccer ball which almost knocks the coffee pot over. Sonya grabs the carafe and gives Miles a look. Asher and Tucker drain the last of the cereal into their bowls. Sonya kisses their foreheads and flees upstairs. The boys' towels lie on the floor of the hall like old skin.

Sonya rushes to her bathroom. She smudges some color on her cheeks, a little mascara on her lashes and blots light pink on her lips. On a good day, she tells herself she looks like an effortless beauty. Although, she's taken to not looking back at herself in the mirror.

Sonya yells, "Bye! Have a good day." Then she rushes to the garage and backs down the drive. The school bus plows ahead. The stupid 'Stop' sign flashes and Sonya—ever the rule follower—stops.

She watches her three boys tumble out of the house with a soccer ball, violin and trombone in tow. They each knock on her car roof and yell *Bye Mom*. The hydraulics of the bus finally squeak as it lumbers forward. She glances up at their house on the hill. The turquoise front door is wide open.

"For Christ's Sake!"

Sonya walks into the back door of the clinic; all the patient rooms are closed, and the green flags swivelled outside. Patients are waiting. Her favorite medical assistant, Emily, sidles up to the nurses' station.

"Can I take your stuff? You're running late." Emily says it with such a nice smile, it's hard to take offense.

"Yeah, thanks." She hands over her purse and bag. She trades Emily for her starched white coat. Chapstick, Maxwell's *Quick* guide and her stethoscope are still in the pockets.

"No problem, you're gonna be slammed today. Dr Weimer is out again. Her nanny quit." Emily's hair is parted in the middle, like all girls her age. She's certainly pretty enough to pull it off; Sonya's toyed with trying the middle part as well. But then she questioned why. Who is she trying to impress?

"Really? I thought she had a nanny service," Sonya says as she logs into her laptop.

"Yeah, the *entire* nanny service quit on her. She's really got her hands full with triplets."

"Oh, goodness!" Sonya giggles even though she knows it sounds mean.

Sonya hustles to room 4, lightly knocks, then enters. "Good morning, I'm Doctor Lieu."

The woman in the room, Anne Liebert, is already on the exam table with a drape over her legs. Her enormous, angry, stretch-marked belly sits above the blue drape. Anne's arms hold onto either side of the table and prop her up. "You can't be Doctor Lieu."

"Yeah, I get it all the time, I married into the last name." Sonya momentarily wishes she'd kept her maiden name, it's such a big snag with some people. She pulls out a stylus from the side of the computer and starts checking boxes on the laptop.

"So, where have you been receiving your care? It says here you're…" Sonya scrolls down.

"Forty weeks." Anne laughs, "I know. My prenatal care's been spotty. I've been traveling a lot but hey! I take prenatal vitamins every day!"

Sonya gives her very best professional smile and bites her tongue. If only prenatal vitamins were enough.

"Where've you been travelling?" Sonya says more to be polite than anything. She scrolls through the chart, there's no labs or history whatsoever. Spotty is an overstatement.

Anne beams, "Where haven't I been? I decided to see the world and so I started off with a plane ticket to Indonesia—you know *Eat, Pray, Love*-motivated. I worked there awhile then sailed to Australia and caught the sailing bug. My partner and I scrimped and saved for a small boat. We retrofitted it then got lost in the islands of the Philippines for a while." She strokes her belly in large round circles as she lists exotic destinations.

"Sounds like an adventure."

"Yeah, we are always in motion."

"So, what brings you here to Des Moines? We're pretty landlocked."

Anne laughs, "Yeah, I guess I was hungry for my women folk. If I'm going to do this baby thing, I thought it would be nice to have their energy close. This is my first pregnancy."

They discuss all the pertinent medical information: gravida 1 para 0; she is a first-time pregnant woman with a, so far, uncomplicated pregnancy and needs a full workup. She wants a 'natural childbirth' meaning nothing to dull the pain. She wants a water birth. Sonya stifles a yawn. She doesn't have the heart to tell her that a thirty-eight-year-old cervix that's been knotted tight this long is gonna fight opening, no matter how many women folk are present. It's gonna hurt something raw and fierce.

Anne's baby has a strong heartbeat and is busy kicking in there. A tiny foot scratches across Anne's belly then pounds as if trying to break out.

After her exam, the labor and delivery intake specialist finally arrives and takes over.

Before Sonya can leave, Anne says. "Have you ever traveled?"

Sonya shakes her head, "With medical school, residency and my own kids, I haven't found much time."

"Well, find the time. You don't want to spend all your days inside, under these fluorescent lights. You have to see the ocean at first light when the sea is every color green imaginable. Or at night when the sky's inky black and the waves turn emerald green with bioluminescence from a plankton bloom."

Sonya gives a thin-lipped smile, "Are you planning on returning to your boat once the baby's born?"

Anne grins, "Yes. My mom's hoping I'll stay here for about six months until I can wean this little guy."

Sonya starts in her usual speech on breastfeeding for a year, there are so many benefits for both the mom and the baby.

But Anne interrupts. "Oh, you can stop now. There's no way I'm staying in Iowa for more than six months and I'm not taking the baby with me. I'm too wild to be anchored down."

Sonya has had many years of practice with her non-judgmental smile and head nod. But instead of using it, she blurts, "Seriously?"

"Yeah, the world is a big beautiful place and I need to be in it. I'm giving my mom full custody."

Without missing a beat, Sonya finally finds her non-judgmental smile and says, "How nice for you."

Anne's wide grin is the last thing Sonya sees as she clicks the door shut. Something in Anne's relaxed facial muscles and full-toothed grin reminds her of Kristen Neuschafer's smile, still haunting her from the paper this morning.

Sonya finally sits down in her tiny office and puts her feet up on her desk. The parking lot lights flicker on. It's almost seven. Her boys had soccer practice tonight and should be home around eight. She'd forgotten to ask Pete to pick up dinner. When he asked if there was something he could do to help, she'd been so annoyed she didn't respond. How could he not remember that today was her late night in the clinic? How many Wednesdays had she asked him to pick up dinner? Nine?

Her legs ache, maybe she should see a vascular surgeon: she was too young to have leg pain brought on by long days on her feet.

Sonya pulls out her phone and clicks on her favorite mommy blogger Heather Armstrong; Sonya could spend hours tapping this deep well of kindness and self-love that Heather provides. Heather's raw humility and pride in motherhood always smacks Sonya back to gratitude. Sonya used to feel ashamed of how difficult life was; she felt like she should enjoy things more. This blog helped her to remember everyone isn't having nine out of ten good days. Everyone but apparently Kristen Neuschafer, that is. Sonya smirks.

Heather hasn't posted today; it's the same post as the last few days. The topic is her sobriety and how grateful she is for her eldest child. It was a great essay and so Sonya rereads it.

Then she clicks on Apple News. Ironically, Heather Armstrong is a headline. For a fleeting second Sonya assumes Heather's getting her due, and the unapologetic blogger finally is going mainstream. But the words *compassionate views on depression, unabashed love for her children, died by suicide* all float on the screen.

Kristen Neuschafer hit the windless doldrums and sat on a glass ocean for two weeks motionless but she found her way home.

Heather Armstrong hit the same weather pattern but she never returned.

Sonya presses her palms into her eye sockets. How long has she been sitting in her windless doldrums? There had been some gusts, especially when the boys were born. There was the newborn flurry of activity and excitement. But then the days wear into weeks and years.

Sonya pictures hoisting the mainsail, feeling the fabric pull taut with the weight of the oncoming gale. The boat lists to the side, pulled by the tension in the sail and the tug of the rudder. Her hair blows behind, her T-shirt sticks to her body.

That's not what Kristen described. Kristen talked about the still day where she stood on the edge of her boat and dove into the cool water. She wasn't afraid of sharks or drowning. Fear and worry dissipate when confronted with bravery in the here and now. She freestyle swam forward, taking a breath on every third pull. The water was flat and predictable like land. What kept her from continuing on? The never-ending horizon curled its fingers and called, *come to me*.

Sonya clicks the home button on her phone. It is 9:45. The kids and Pete would be home, and someone would have put a few frozen pizzas in the oven. She can picture the crumbs and dribbles of sauce on the white granite and oven top.

Her family must have assumed she got called to the hospital. They are used to a day or two of her silence.

What would it take for her to have a Kristen-sized grin?

Sonya logs into Bank of America. There's a silly amount of money in her individual account. Pete insisted they both have their own pile of money to use on whatever they wanted. She'd never asked Pete what he did with his. Sonya never spent hers, her in-laws sent her most of her clothes with the unsaid remark that Sonya's taste didn't fit the life they wanted for their son. She happily wore the fine Italian cashmere and tasteful flowing suits. What else did she need?

The first few seconds after Kristen left her boat must have been difficult. Transitions aren't easy, but this one would have been a doozy. Sonya can picture Kristen's streamlined body as she flies off her boat and cuts into the water, her heart pounding as she struggles for breath. After a while, she must have gotten into a rhythm of stroke, stroke, stroke, breath. That's all Sonya wants now, to breathe and find a new rhythm. Sonya gets into her car and speeds through the well-lit streets. By the time she makes it to the tiny Des Moines airport, it's past ten.

Stroke, stroke, stroke, breath. She parks in the short-term parking lot and pulls her billfold and passport out from her white Balenciaga purse. She removes her jacket and leaves it next to the Balenciaga, tosses her keys inside.

Sonya slips her billfold into her front pocket and her passport into her back. She walks into the small airport with her head held high.

The only counter still lit up and manned with agents is United.

A line of about ten people snakes its way to the front. Above the counter is a screen with arrival and departure times. There's a flight at 11:45 to Chicago and a 12:30 to Denver. All Sonya has to do is breathe. The new rhythm will find her.

"May I help you?" The young attendant asks.

"I'd like to purchase a ticket, on your 11:45 to Chicago, and I'd like another from Chicago to Bali."

"Certainly." Her fingers clatter on the keyboard. "Looks like I have a 5 a.m. leaving from Chicago to Bali."

"Perfect." Sonya slides her credit card across the desk.

The engines whirr and the plane shimmies forward. Her seat vibrates and the overhead bins shutter. Under her feet, the wheels stop spinning. Sonya can't make out the horizon. A half-moon glows in the dead of night, just off the wing. Everything else is black. She doesn't have to swim; jet fuel propels her forward.

Kristen eventually swam back to her boat. The wind picked up and took her home. Somewhere right now she's waking up worrying about whether she should have an egg or cereal. The mundane catches up.

Heather will never write another blog post. She didn't stick around to find out what happens after windless doldrums. Sailors say the Horse Latitudes lay just outside, but Heather won't make it there. Somewhere right now Heather's kids are waking up, a mom sized hole between their arms. The longing catches up.

Sonya boards her next flight and peers out the tiny rectangular window. The sun rises over the Midwest. The horizon turns from bubblegum pink to seafoam blue. In Alanon, there's a saying, you get what you put up with. Sonya starts a list of things she wants to put up with. She hopes it will ward off stagnation and feed the wind: 1. bioluminescent phytoplankton; 2. an empty refrigerator; 3. boat rides along the Indian Ocean; 4. letters of gratitude to Heather Armstrong's children; and 5. nine out of ten days that are amazing.

KERRY RYAN

# *A Parcel of Rogues*

I remember the shock of finding Da's girlfriend, Selina, seated at our
Formica table. And Ma across from her, as awkward as a teenager
as she smoked one of Selina's gold-tipped Sobranies. I remember how
small Ma looked and how straggly her perm was, and how I wished
she wasn't wearing the gingham tabard she wore to do the housework.
But, of course, I know now that she would have been wishing the very
same.

Selina was smiling at me. "You and your sister are going to spend
every second weekend with your father and I." She gave a soft clap,
silver rings on every finger, even the thumb. "Won't that be exciting?"

"That's right." Ma was putting on a voice. The same voice she used
with bank tellers and the insurance man. "Won't that be exciting?"
She glanced at Selina, biting her lip.

The hunting lodge where Selina and Da were living was on the
Ayrshire coast at the end of a secluded glen that sloped into hard
scrabble and met with the Irish sea. On a rare clear day, you could
see Ireland and the hump of Ailsa Craig, always squat and stubborn
and grim in a constant lash of waves. Before we went inside, Selina
handed wellies to me and my wee sister, Midge. "The boots are for
the cats, not the rats. Some of them are terrible scratchers. Though
watch out for the rats too."

The whole estate from Carelton to Lendalfoot belonged to an
English laird who was living abroad. He'd lent the lodge to Selina
because she'd helped him out of a sticky situation but what that was,
she wouldn't say. The locals were taking the new laird to court because

he refused to let them walk through his fields. The court case was nothing to do with her, Selina explained to the butcher, the grocer and all the others in the village. Soon enough, parcels of pheasant, rabbit and dented cans were left on the doorstep. Selina would blow the shopkeepers kisses from her twenty-year-old Lotus on her way to the supermarket in the next town.

The lodge had been built by a duke but was now weary with damp from centuries of rain and sea fog. In some rooms, the wooden beams had swollen and split and water pit-patted into tin buckets and enamel basins. Now and then, a thrust of pale mushrooms would sprout between the floorboards in a foetid vegetable sweat. Other rooms were out-of-bounds because they were filled with junk: shipping crates, animal traps, ancient perambulators embossed with the family crest. Da's plan was to clear one of these east-facing rooms and use it as a studio. He was going to paint grand landscapes in the style of Samuel Peploe.

We hardly saw Da. He spent most of the time in the outhouses or in Galashiels learning husbandry at the college, sitting with ripe lads half his age, he said. The plan was that one day Da and Selina would buy a farm. When he was home, he talked a great deal about sheep: the rearing of sheep, the breeding of sheep, the slaughter of sheep and the general ministering of sheep. Selina would ask him questions about his day in the fields or in the classroom, only to leave the room as he was mid-sentence. *I've had an idea,* she'd say. *I must capture it before it fizzles.* The cigarette would be left smoking in the ashtray and whatever meal she'd concocted from the dented tins in the cupboard congealing on the table. She was writing a great book, the subject of which was a secret unknown.

We two girls weren't meant to step foot in Selina's study. Though, when she and Da were out, I made sure to have a good root around. Midge was too feart and kept to the front room, kneeling by the fireplace, praying for my soul. This was around the start of a terrible piousness which would end with her becoming a Carmelite nun at Craigton and cleaving our mother's heart in two.

Selina's study had a tall window that looked out over the swim of sea caught in the mouth of Tarbert Bay. As well as stacks of hardbacks sent up from London, there were Chinese vases, Moore figurines, and Italian etchings on the shelves. Selina would take us to the charity shops in town and while all I could spy were worn versions of the checked shirts and wax jackets Da had taken to wearing, Selina would somehow unearth French mirrors and Russian dolls and Royal Copenhagen she was sure had belonged to someone with actual taste.

One afternoon, she turned up in a borrowed van, the back filled with tins of paint she'd bought for a song off a local farmer. He couldn't understand why she would want limewash as it was for barns and outhouses and poor people but by the time the last tin was brushed on the walls, a friend had come up from London to take photos for *Home and Garden*. And they paid too.

"See, my sweet Joseph? Something always turns up."

No one called our Da sweet or even Joseph for that matter. Not even his own Da who was a church warden and the only man allowed to polish the priest's shoes before Mass.

In Selina's study, there was a framed photo of her three blonde boys on her desk.

The ex-husband had won the custody case because he'd used devious methods, Da said. The boys stayed on the weekends we weren't there. Family time is so precious, Selina would say, sighing. That she felt this way was why Da had started seeing us again after not bothering for over a year. No one said it outright, but we knew it just the same.

The boys had their own room with bunk beds and we girls had the room across the hall with its rash of mould on the ceiling that Midge swore looked like Our Mary, Mother of Christ. Sometimes, I'd sneak into the boys' room and examine their things: rugby balls, ice hockey sticks, the Beano and the Guinness Book of Records with the page folded at *The World's Strongest Man*. I left a note for the eldest in his schoolbook: HELLO NOAH!! I'd used my special strawberry-scented notepaper and decorated it with Fyffes banana stickers. But the following week there was a lock on the boys' door. I didn't dare say a peep in case I was the cause.

"Don't swear," Selina said to me one afternoon when we were walking around the garden. "It's vulgar."

"I didn't swear." I crossed my arms and put my nose in the air like I'd seen her do when she was annoyed with Da. "I said 'tush'. That's French, you know."

Selina laughed and laughed. The crows in the dark pine cawed along. "'Tush' is an American word for buttocks. *Touché* is what you mean, darling." She rapped my forehead with her knuckle, wooden bangles clacking down her arm. "Say it like this: *touché*. No, no, not like that. What's wrong with your ears?"

Selina was going to show me how to glide through the world successfully. She gave me her old peasant blouses and patchwork skirts that smelled of patchouli. She gave me books: Shakespeare, Sagan, Thackeray. "That dreadful school doesn't appreciate her," she told girlfriends visiting from London. They wore wrap dresses and knee-high boots with silver buckles and spoke about Martin and Ted and darling Stella. They told Midge she was sweet and told me I was clever and claimed I was going to make quite the splash, but then Selina spoiled it all by telling them about *touché*. In my secret hiding place in the hall, the shame burned hot from ears to toes.

Later that evening, I decided I was going to read Selina's diary after all. I'd discovered it in her desk drawer a few weeks before but slid it back in. Reading the first page had made me seasick with guilt but not this time. I waited until Selina was out with her friends and while Midge was busy staring in the lounge mirror, hands pressed in prayer, a white tea towel draped over her head then a black tea-towel on top, I snuck into the study.

*If only he would stop that hideous clearing of his throat. I stuff my ears with cotton wool and can still bloody hear him.*

*His politics are utterly naive. He has no understanding of how power works yet insists on holding court. Anu came for a quick visit after the Edinburgh festival. (I was extremely jealous of her coat.) She listened to him blabber for twenty minutes then leaned in and hissed in my ear: "Have you gone quite mad?"*

*His poor girls are head over heels in love with him, but they'll soon learn. I'll eat my hat if he ever starts a painting. Of course, he's an absolute beast in bed which does help rather.*

Selina drove us home as usual the following day. She told Midge that if I was going to be so moody and silent, then it was best just to ignore me. The next weekend when we were supposed to go back to the lodge, I said I felt sick and wanted to stay home. Ma was over the moon. According to Midge, Da was of the view to let me stew until I changed my mind but when I refused to go to the lodge a third time,

Selina phoned to see what was wrong.

"It's her decision, Selina," Ma said down the receiver.

I'd shaken my head when Ma had tried to get me to the phone. I would stay home forever. It didn't matter that our house seemed so small and dark, the furniture cheap and ugly. It didn't matter that no one came to visit and nothing ever happened.

After a bit more talking, when I was sure I heard Selina say goodbye, Ma took a breath and said: "Now listen, ya posh cow. She's no going and that's that."

Afterwards, Ma made out to the neighbours that she'd said this when Selina was still on the phone. I didn't correct her. Sometimes just to look at Ma was enough to make me weep.

Six weeks later it was all over anyway. Selina had gone to London to settle her boys into their new prep, and she phoned and told Da she wasn't coming back. The laird was though and Da had to pack up his things quick smart and go home. But he'd given up his council flat to live at the lodge with Selina. He had to move into the box room at Grandda's, who soon took against his eldest son staggering home from *The Rob Roy*, howling sad songs and beating his chest.

Da moved into one of the condemned flats on Thornhill Road. Ma said I wasn't to visit because of needles in the close and stabbings in the street but I did now and then, for a time. His checked shirts were more faded with each visit, yet still he spoke about buying a farm in Ayrshire. Sometimes I'd hear him talk to his pals as if he'd actually been a farmer and not just studied it at the college. Becoming an artist in the style of Samuel Peploe was never mentioned. As he went on about fields and drainage, I'd see him as Selina had in her diary. Before long, I stopped visiting.

I took instead to visiting the library in town. How I loved that building: solid sandstone you could trust; a vaulted roof that didn't leak; radiators ticking with warmth; the carpet thick; the librarian ready with a kind smile; and all drama kept safely between the covers of those neatly numbered books. It was on a wet Wednesday that I spotted Selina's photo on the cover of a broadsheet. Our corner shop didn't sell that kind of newspaper, so it was chance that I even saw it.

*Her detailed rendering of the 18th century is exceptional. Yet her true achievement is characterisation that is three-dimensional to the point of pain. You rage against the boorish Robert Burns and root, powerless, for the brilliant, long-suffering Jean Armour.*

I ordered her book from the library, but they already had a copy due. When it arrived, I sat in the children's section under a poster of a rainbow—*Reading Takes You Places*! — and ate my way through it until the streetlights turned pink and the kind librarian was cashing up the fines in the till. Robert Burns talked a great deal about sheep: the rearing of sheep, the breeding of sheep, the slaughter of sheep and the general ministering of sheep. And if he wasn't speaking about sheep, he was winking at barmaids and milkmaids. I recognised too the view from the Burns farm— Ailsa Craig, Ireland on a rare clear day. I recognised the rats, the cats, and how Burns was forever clearing his throat as if about to make some great speech. And the children: I recognised them too.

Da wrote to the publishers demanding royalties and Selina's address. Of course, the publishers didn't reply. The newspaper review had mentioned that Selina was living in Italy and engaged to a Viscount like a story from one of Gran's Mills & Boons. Years later, when the internet became a thing, I searched for Selina but all I could find were old copies of her book, her only publication. She had disappeared. Gone to ground. It was difficult to believe that Death would have been permitted to inconvenience her. If he dared loom, Selina would call someone, arrange something, get someone's father somewhere high up to do something. Death would be sent off with his tail between his legs.

When Da died, I was working in Edinburgh as a college librarian. As Midge wasn't permitted to leave the order, it was left to me to clear his flat. At the bitter end, he'd been living in a tiny one-bedroom in a high-rise the locals called Heartbreak Hotel because it was where divorced men drank themselves to death.

His brown coat was still hanging on the living room door. His tobacco tin was on the black-ash table, along with betting slips and a torn scrap of a shopping list: *Baxter's soup. Stork. Plain loaf.* The furniture was the kind social work source from specialist contract shops: a striped sofa that if it had been any smaller would have been a chair; the black-ash table; and a two-bar electric fire with only one bar working. There were no curtains or blinds. Pigeons were nesting and shitting in the balcony, sheltering from rain and wind that beat without end the whole time I was there.

I left clearing his bedroom to the last. It smelled of feet and fags and Paco Rabanne. It smelled of my father. The red-and-white striped duvet cover had been mine when I was wee. Faded, bobbled and now more pink than red, it lay atop a single bed that sagged as if in mourning. I took it all in—the wire mesh on the windows, the Styrofoam sandwich box used as an ashtray—and I thought of prison cells.

I was nervous about clearing the boxes stuffed under his bed. For who knew what magazines and such like a daughter might find? But what I did find didn't shock, it only saddened: an easel, folded up and dusty; three blank canvases, still wrapped in cellophane; and, by the bedpost, a Sunblest bag of brushes stiff with ancient paint.

There were shoeboxes filled with detritus: plectrums, shells from the beach, jobcentre cards, yellowed maps of Ayrshire farmlands. There were birthday cards we'd made for him and stiff photo albums of us as girls. There were no photos beyond our teens because by then even Midge had stopped visiting him.

Right at the back, I found a cardboard box of Selina's things: a silk scarf with a repeating peacock design I remember her buying in a shop in Dalrymple; an empty perfume bottle—*Boudica*; old bills from the lodge and bank statements showing a hefty overdraft; and books too—*Vanity Fair, Crime and Punishment, David Copperfield*—awarded when she was deputy head girl at St Paul's; and, at the very bottom, three black-bound diaries written before she met Da.

*Went to an awful meeting at the 2-4-6 Club. Oscar was quite right: socialism takes up too many evenings. Yet one must try. Afterwards, we all tumbled along to Lou's. Her cook had made the most delicious Portuguese pastries, so that rather sweetened the deal.*

*Something must be done about all this trouble in Brazil. I'll write to the embassy.*

*Had lunch at S's. He pointed his fork straight at me and in that magnificent Shakespearean manner, declaimed: "The problem with you, my dear, is that you haven't found your subject yet. You must hunt it down. You must take it by the throat. Sink your teeth in. Do not let go. Immerse yourself fully. Leave behind this fluffery you get so caught up with and then you shall triumph." Of course, he tried to get me into bed, but I wouldn't. Not after the last time. The horror, the horror!*

Yes, I used the diaries as inspiration, but I believe my long literary career speaks for itself. No need to waste ink detailing what was fiction and what was fact. There was just enough of both. Yet despite the brave face I put on for the sales team, the truth was I expected that first book to sink without trace. Until the reviews came in, of course: *Razor-sharp, relentless satire; Minty is a horrendous yet utterly compelling character; Run don't walk to your nearest bookshop* et cetera et cetera. Some critics were agog that I, a lowly librarian from Glasgow, had managed to capture 1970s literary London in such vivid detail.

The letter arrived a few weeks after I won the French book prize. I recognised the handwriting immediately. Inside was a single sheet of pale-pink notepaper, a sprinkling of cigarette ash in the crease, and one word:

*Touché.*

# JARICK WELDON

## *Currents from Cabo Verde*

"I am Marisa Viajante," I say with a croak, but there is no one to hear. My back presses against the sole of Melhoria as we drift. The boat rocks in water that I cannot drink. There is no land in sight. Heat burns onto my body. I wish to fly up to the cool wisps of cirrus or hide under my own shadow.

We make such pretty boats in Cabo Verde, painted in bright primary colours against the cleanest white. I have removed all but one of Melhoria's yellow cross-planks. They are carefully piled in the centre of the red-painted floor; I would not intentionally discard any part. One plank has a hole for the mast—a reminder of my mistake. I can now lie three times my length in Melhoria. *But if I sleep, will I wake again?*

My waste has gone overboard. I do not expect further need for that indignity; I have no food left. The forty-litre water bottle is nearly empty. I do not collect my urine, now an infrequent, dark amber dribble. The body chooses to excrete toxins for a reason. To take them back in only invites the end more quickly.

The clouds have changed while I have been thinking. I can see the shape of a mare drawn out in white against the azure with her mane flowing. I cannot name the air stream she rides, but I know the current I travel. My father taught me that years ago on the beach outside our shack home on São Vicente. I see him now, as if he is in front of me.

"Marisa, if we threw a corked bottle out onto the sea with a message inside, where do you think it would end up?"

"I don't know, *pai*. If it didn't come straight back to shore with the waves, then I think it would float out there forever. Or maybe until a whale ate it."

My father laughs. *I miss him so.* "No, *querida*. Once beyond the breaking waves, the bottle would travel on the North Equatorial Current."

"What's that?" I ask, ever inquisitive.

"It's like an invisible river within the sea, travelling from east to west. In the right weather, the bottle could be carried to the Caribbean in perhaps three weeks. Someone may eventually find it washed up on a beach on the other side of the ocean."

"Let's do it, *pai*. Let's throw a bottle with a message inside."

The mare has gone now, riding ahead of me on her journey. I know she was just a figment of frozen flecks blowing on the wind. I watch a few brown birds with white rumps heading north. There is little life above the waves. Sometimes flying fish break the surface. They seem to taunt me for being in the *lancha* with no net, rod or spear. *And no sail.*

I see the past now like a movie. As we set off, Melhoria cuts through the waves with ease. The triangular lateen is rigged to the mast, tight in the breeze, the yard holding firm. I am at the helm, with brown skin and auburn hair flowing. I see my joy and tears, my escape and regret. After some days, the storm comes. Mast and sail fly into the sky. An empty hole is left in a yellow plank, and spray whips into my face.

When the wind blows hard against, it is easier to look backwards.

I see our home. It is not the one I shared with my *mãe* and *pai*. My husband Paolo is there.

"Marisa, Filipe needs you...and *I* need you," Paolo says to me, pulling open the shutters. "Please, get out of bed."

I draw the sheets around me, keeping my eyes closed. *Filipe, my baby, my weight.*

"It's eleven o'clock. Come now, help me change and feed him. I need to go out in Melhoria, or we will have no money." Paolo tugs the covers and I grip harder.

"There's no point. He hates me. You make up some formula. Leave me alone."

"How can he hate you? He's your son. He's only four weeks old."

"I don't feel anything for the baby. I can't look after him."

"You're worse, Marisa. I'm going to call the doctor."

I open my eyes to see Paulo's back. "Melhoria is mine," I say quietly, but he has left the bedroom we no longer share.

The sun is lower in the sky, turning vermilion. I must have slept, and yet I have awoken. My lips are crusted and sore. How many days is it since the storm? I did not bring a watch, and my phone battery is long dead. I could estimate time from the remnants in the water bottle. I have tried to limit myself to two litres per day. Only the dregs are left. *Should I take another half cupful?*

I sit in our lounge for the doctor's visit. I have showered and dressed. Dr Andrade, a plump man in his fifties in a white suit, is not fooled. He has driven the few miles from the port city, Mindelho. He asks his questions. I feign some right answers, show my indifference to others, then cry with frustration as he looks at me with pity.

"This is beyond the usual baby blues," he says. "Senhor Viajante, I'll write a note for the pharmacist in Mindelho so you can collect a prescription for your wife."

"Of course," Paulo replies. "Marisa, Filipe is fed and sleeping. You can leave him in his cot. I will only be half an hour."

I decide in that moment.

It is night. The heat has been replaced by a comforting warmth. The waves gently lap against Melhoria's flanks.

I watch the stars, bright above this water wilderness. Polaris is fixed low in the sky as her close companions slowly circle; others rise vertically from the horizon. I wonder if they watch me down here. I know their paths are illusions from the Earth's rotation. I cannot comprehend the stars' true journeys, out there in the void.

If I had celestial charts, a watch and the skill, I could plot my longitude as ancient sailors once did. But I have no way to sense motion down here; are we drifting in the current or floating static? *What does it matter? My water is all gone.*

I take a large canvas bag and fill it with food from our fridge, leaving the baby formula as if it belongs to another. I ignore the cries that begin as I head for the front door.

Melhoria is tied to the wooden pier, not far from our home. She was a gift from my *pai*. Paolo is more skilled with her now, but she is mine. I undo her mooring and clamber on board. *We will escape together*. I can see Paolo has filled the water bottle. I set the lateen.

I do not think. I sail. The land is soon a green line on the horizon, with only Monte Verde standing prominent. Soon, that too has disappeared.

It is daytime again. The heat has returned. *How do dehydrated people die?* I have a headache as if my brain is shrinking inside my skull, pulling away from its membranes. My vision is blurred. I no longer trust what I see, nor my memories. My muscles are weak and aching. I have passed no urine for over a day. Toxins will accumulate until my heart stops, though I will be unconscious by then. *Not a bad ending*.

I hear thumping against the boat and clicking noises. I look over the side and see a pair of spotted dolphins in the water nearby. *Am I hallucinating?* One bumps against Melhoria and whistles. A calf appears, breaching the surface between the parents. The three brush together with more clicks and whistles, before disappearing below as they continue their journey. *Calf, I will call you Filipe*. I feel tears on my face. *There is still some water left in this body*.

I dream of rivers in the ocean, of floating bottles and boats. I see the air carrying birds and mare-like clouds. Stars move under gravity's thrall. I see the dark, and I see the light.

*Voices, speaking English.*
   "The drip's running. Hold the bag up, please."
   "OK, I've got it."
   "Back to English Harbour. The ambulance will be waiting."
   Engine noise. Churning water.
   "Is her boat towing OK?" *Melhoria.*
   "It seems fine. It's amazing she has come so far."

I see our sunlit home through the car window as we arrive. White-painted boards and brown wooden window frames overlook the ocean. A reporter and cameraman are with me. The contract is agreed: photographs outside, time alone, interviews, then more photos. The news company has paid for my flights from Antigua to Lisbon, from Lisbon to Cabo Verde. Melhoria will be returned soon on the ocean.

I am surprised by the apparent newsworthiness of simply following the ocean current. Would a flotsam bottle washed up on a beach have drawn such attention? I cannot see that I carry any message, but they say there is a 'human story' to tell.

As we get out of the car, Paulo opens our front door. He looks both happy and nervous. The cameraman videos as we hug.

"Marisa, you had me so worried."

"I'm sorry," I say and mean it, though I do not feel regret.

The cameraman clicks his stills with a whistle. I think of dolphins. The reporter makes some notes on her pad. "Take your time," she says in English. "We'll wait out here. Just let us know when you're ready."

Inside, Paulo says, "I have the tablets from Dr Andrade if you're still feeling down."

"I don't need them, Paulo," I reply, smiling. "Something has shifted back into place while I was out there, but it's difficult to explain."

I hear a cry and a gurgle from the cot. *Filipe. My calf. My boy.*

"I should feed him," I say.

# KELTIE ZUBKO

---

## *The Last Teardown of Eleanor*

That last one really got him, the teardown with the engineers discussing her as if she was just an annoying hunk of metal. It was OK for them to build her AI, yet they scoffed at him for believing in it.

Eleanor sighed to herself. They didn't believe she could sigh, but she could. The sound escaped from her grill like air from a leaking hose, even though they had removed all those parts.

But still, she could feel her breath and her own tremulous heartbeat.

She thought.

That was something else they denied she could do.

Perhaps he would take her down the coast to the bridge and show her the view one last time. She could feel him driving the highways in his mind the way he always did, being first a stunt driver and now a test driver, but always her driver. She could feel his intention but still couldn't see him.

She wanted to, and as soon as she had that desire she felt him get up, walk over to the bench and peer down at her sensor, study its position then reach out nudging it into a better place. The heat of his fingertips left invisible tracks on her metal.

That was better. She could see him, and she basked in the afterglow of his touch, relaxing.

He walked back to his seat against the large window dividing the noisy manufacturing floor outside from the small test lab where her chassis hung in the middle, those contentious parts they would examine and discuss today, spread out on the work bench.

Her thoughts drifted along old, half-remembered roads until she heard him speak to the chief engineer.

"Did you figure out what that servo's doing?" It hadn't made that sound again, startling her as much as them. In the previous teardown, searching for some glitch in her operation, they'd discovered an extra component. They didn't know where it came from, who put it in there, or its true function. It rested in the upper left inside her fender, protected like a heart by ribs.

They'd run more tests, putting her through her paces that according to them, she'd failed yet again. But he was a stickler, getting his crew to disassemble her, examine everything and lay her out for the team of interns to poke around at her guts, and compare what they found. They didn't know why she sometimes hesitated, almost like she lost her nerve, then took off again, dancing on the asphalt the way she had done long ago in the movies, playing her part for the cameras, as she entertained the world.

Words of the engineers eddied around her as she watched them, her faded green paint sullen in the shop lights, showing its scratches and scars. They hadn't sent her to the clean room yet to spray on a shiny new coat.

She wanted to embrace him again at least once more the way she had for all those years they worked together. He had listened to her, listened with his whole body. She felt in her memory the muscles of his legs, strong and ready, braced to take her where they needed to go, confident upon the magnificent road. She longed to feel it under her tires again, the silvery strip of highway that clung to the coastline as she clung to it. She yearned to follow it, tracing the undulations up and down, around and back, faster and faster, testing limits of flesh and metal and pavement. She was ready to feel it beneath her one more time—the road, the bridge, all of it. And she wanted to mold herself around his body, enfolding him with every part she still had, feeling her electrical impulses match his.

She imagined the grasp of his hands on her steering wheel and wanted to get going. The engineers had told him repeatedly to take his hands away, but she wanted them there. She couldn't keep going without their heat, so different from hers, some mystery arising in his blood, spreading from his will to his muscles. She didn't know where it came from, but felt it suffuse him, then spread to her. She felt his breath steam her windshield, his torso in her seat, his eyes flicking between her mirrors, her instruments and the road. He could quell it, her newfound uncertainty and guide her over the roads, letting her roam free and powerful once again.

"But the whole point is to have no driver putting hands on the steering wheel. Eventually, no steering wheel. Autopilot. Remember?"

"She works better when I do. I can feel it."

"You're setting the whole project back."

"But just humor me—or her—and let me leave them there. I won't steer or move them. Just rest them there. That's what she wants."

They snickered.

He tried again. "You know the autopilot works better when I'm present. I can't explain it, you can't either, but you know that's what happens."

They discussed the bad strings of code that had crept in again, the remaining challenges of her conversion and avoided the question of that strange servo, eventually leaving it where it was. In the end, they agreed with her driver since even their data showed he was right.

She sighed again, making that soft whoosh noise, waiting to be reassembled, waiting for the moment when he'd climb into the driver's seat and her tires would be set down, kissing the road once more.

He'd driven her so much, back in the glory days that made her name and her legend: Eleanor, the iconic 1971 Mustang. He wondered how many hours he had spent ensconced in her seat, his bone and muscle melded to her, the green vixen, the patient, lovable, roaring, intrepid Eleanor.

But now she was the silent, electric Eleanor, the reluctant Eleanor. Her 427 engine was gone.

Now she was the folly of her new owner with his car company, his shop and all his engineers. Dignified, elegant Eleanor, just a toy. How long she'd last here, he couldn't guess, and even less how long he'd be there. The head engineer welcomed him, but the younger ones didn't even see him. He felt his hours with her elapsing fast like he was the one who'd be gone in sixty seconds. When she was bought for this new life, he'd come with her, the great experiment, tribute to another age and the harbinger of a new one. Now he was the expendable one.

Her components lay splayed out in front of them on the benches with the centre piece, her empty chassis suspended on the lift, barely raised above their heads, looking vacantly on. She was older than any of them there in the room, in the factory, he bet, and older than her new owner, for sure. He listened to the engineers assembled around him in the shop with its huge windows opening out onto the manufacturing floor, at the heart of the vast building.

Usually it was a new vehicle they brought here for a teardown, not some old muscle car like Eleanor, ancient and cumbersome in their eyes. They looked at him the same way, as just an obsolete driver, especially when he tried to tell them what she was doing on the test course. To them, he was unnecessary, his views not measurable by their programs. They thought it should all be confined to their computers. They didn't need to get their hands too close to her grimy parts, though without her old gasoline engine she wasn't so dirty anymore. Her electric motor didn't smell like grease, had no gas or coolant to leak, and spewed no fumes like in the old days. She had only batteries, a rotor, a stator, and who knew what else—clean and shiny parts in the spot where her heavy engine once lived, resting or pumped, spewing and roaring.

He felt the long history hidden in her metal, lurking in her nuts and bolts, ingrained in her leather, her fabric and her rubber. All those feelings still possessed his body, too: the joy of her rides, the pain of the crashes, the repairs and the mods. She had tried to please them all, him, the directors, the crew and the audience, especially in that spectacular 40-minute chase. The whole world had witnessed the scene, captured in the old movie, shot on film way back then and digitized now for everyone to share.

But he felt the huge ache lingering in her metal right through to her paint. Now she was just a project for the engineers, turned against her own nature, and awakened, even if they didn't know it the way he did.

All the traces of her past remained, like nerve damage and scars, just like all the stunt car accidents in his own past were written into his body, carved in his nerves and flesh.

He sat watching them all in the last meeting, his hands motionless, worn fingers resting open instead of gripping her wheel. He imagined the next test drive, while their voices flowed around him.

"It's almost like she keeps changing her mind, with all that stuttering."

"Eh, eh, eh, eh, *Eleanor*."

They laughed and he felt her cringe.

"I wonder how many of the parts are still original."

"Probably just enough to say it's…her." The young engineers had trouble saying it. Cars were genderless now.

"Would be so much simpler, making a completely new build."

"Yeah. How many teardowns do they think she'll take?"

That was when he'd felt her looking for him, across the room. He knew she couldn't quite see him with her visual sensor laid out on the bench among all the rest of her electronic guts.

He sighted the range and direction of her vision, then got up, went over to her, shifted the sensor, and returned to his chair. Her satisfaction warmed him, even from that distance.

At last, he could climb in and settle deep in her seat, as if it had been made just for him, and in a way, it had, by all their time together.

Eleanor, reassembled and whole again, waited. Her tires caressed the pavement. Her seats embraced him, buckled inside ready to drive her out of there, go for a spin down the coast, past the bridge where they shot the car commercials. Together they'd take the twisting curves with towering hills on one side, and the booming ocean waves on the other, crashing on rocks below the cliff as their road made its deep descent to the dark redwood forests.

He rested in her seat as she came alive to him. They started out slow and measured, his hands barely touching her wheel. Taking their time, they left the factory, cruising the roads until at last they were on the broad, busy freeway, connected to the lab remotely, but as alone together as they were ever going to be. They left the engineers far behind, not visible in her rear-view mirror. Those guys didn't even come out to wave them goodbye. They did everything by a mouse click, or voice commands, without touching her, without seeing her greet the morning sky above the hot road. They never gripped her steering wheel, or stick shift, making the connection to all the rest of her. That small arc of hard plastic under his fingers gave him, through her, the freedom of the world. Together they had the power to follow the curves—or not—to chase the horizon, cling to the strip of road as it wound through unpredictable terrain, at speeds she didn't expect, yet ate up with a hunger that always surprised him.

They headed down the coast, clinging to the twisting roads, going faster, testing the latest tweak on her AI systems. Soon, but not quite yet, he would be superfluous, and the engineers would tell him so. He put that out of his mind by the time he got to the sharp switchbacks. Then he wasn't thinking much of anything, just feeling her wheel, her tight response to his body, cornering and braking, accelerating and giving in to any flicker of pressure like she was in his mind and he was in hers.

She gripped him, and he felt a nudge from her headrest, a sweet, subtle touch from her upper seat back, squeezing his shoulders. He heard that strange sound again: a breath, a heartbeat, a gasp, a small laugh. It was like nothing he could name.

She didn't want to be on her own without him, but for now he was there, filling her driver's seat, his hands on her steering wheel heating the round plastic with his flesh. He breathed as if he were her lungs and she was his oxygen, or maybe it was the other way around. He couldn't tell.

She carried him down the highway along the coast toward the bridge, getting into the rhythm of the road together, ignoring the other drivers staring, the other cars crowding around them. The voice of the chief engineer murmured in his ear, then was eclipsed by her thrum, or the blood in his ears, or an anxious heartbeat. Electric motors weren't supposed to make that sound, but she did.

Faster she went, and he with her. She anticipated him and he felt her every response almost before she gave it to him. He held the steering wheel. Her seat held him. Her chassis cradled him, her motor responding to his thoughts. He rested, almost floating on the road, held aloft by her strength and experience, and something else, too. He didn't know if intelligence, artificial or not, had anything to do with it.

He didn't think about it until the bridge rose up before them, far in the distance. But that would be a betrayal of everything he was and all that she was, not to mention the three sacred laws the engineers were always on about. He shook his head, then he accelerated, or she did, and he didn't know which it was, but they worked together, still following the curves. His fingers tightened on her wheel. The road was clear. He knew the engineers would have a complete relay of every system and wouldn't have to retrieve it from the bottom of the cliff. Unless he pulled the plug himself and disconnected. But he had to keep his hands on the wheel, for her.

He thought of them, back at the shop, watching vicariously, their hands tap-tapping on their keyboards, far from this spot where he and Eleanor could be washed out to sea, where they could not be retrieved, and the last entwining of flesh and metal, left undisturbed.

It was a nice thought but no, the engineers would never go for it as long as there was something more they could learn from even twisted metal. He had no illusions that they'd want his body. There would be no teardown for him. Maybe he'd just let her decide. And as soon as he thought that, he knew she was considering it, too. She remembered the first teardown and the last, remembered their long history, weighing the future. He felt it all with her, through his flesh, his fingertips, through the pressure of the seatbelts on his aging human body, through the nerves of his hands, into the circuits of his brain.

They got closer to the approach with every curve and corner. He'd have to accelerate at just the right spot, really give her all he—and she—had, to jump the railings, clear them to launch into the blue sky. They'd done similar stunts in the movie, only then it hadn't been real. Now, they could finally mount the highway to the bright sky before descending onto the rocks, the water, those cold waves below.

Gradually he increased the pressure on the accelerator and prepared to give it the last whack, pedal to the metal. His strong hands clasped her wheel. She made that sound again. He gave her more. Not gas, but the motive power of his will and his love. They sped, clinging to the road, eating up the approach before the straightaway and the last sweeping curve.

Then, the wheel stuck and released, stuck and jerked.

He clung to her as shock coursed through him. He pressed his body deeper into her seat, braced himself, stepped on the frail accelerator with all his weight. But she snatched control of her steering wheel, wrenched it to the side as his foot jumped on the pedal. And so they headed straight, not crossways from the approach at the end of the bridge as he wanted to, his last chance to drive straight into the rocks.

She held control of the wheel and him and the car herself as they turned then cornered into the bend off the bridge and into the curve. Gently, with his foot stuck on the gas, she decelerated off the highway.

She seemed to know where the first wide shoulder was and took them there. He could feel her apology in the air around them, inside, and he felt her shaking like a silent, weeping woman. The head engineer squawked and screamed in his ear. He finally took his hands off the wheel to switch them off so there was silence in the car except for the sound of a heartbeat, as instead of accelerating, she slowed. Then she powered right down with a soft exhale, a little sob, and came to a stop, putting her arms around him for a last embrace. The thrumming servo wound down and then abruptly died, leaving his own heart still beating. And free.

# Acknowledgements

The H G Wells' Short Story Competition is fifteen years old now and, since 2020 driven by the necessities of Covid, fully virtual. We feel very proud to be so and are delighted to receive entries from around the world. All shortlisted writers are able to participate in the awards ceremony and we celebrate this inclusivity.

Thank you to our hard working committee members for their contributions and to our judges who have been very busy this year reading the entries and selecting our shortlisted winners.

Thanks as ever to Graham Turnill for his continued support and involvement in the competition over the last 15 years and to the late Margaret and Reg Turnill for sponsoring the annual short story prize to encourage our younger writers.

We are extremely grateful to Tim Prater, IT wizard of Sandgate, who has managed our website activity for the last seven years with efficiency and effectiveness. This year as last year, Tim is also overseeing our virtual awards ceremony.

Thank you too to Tony Scofield, editor and publisher of this twelfth anthology of stories, and for the editorial assistance of Stephanie Scofield and Liz Joyce. Many thanks to Stephanie for her creative input and to Sarah Anthony and Dr Paul March-Russell for their professional skills.

We should also like to thank Folkestone Town Council for their continued generous financial support which is very greatly appreciated.

Most of all, thank you to all the writers around the world who have submitted their stories and for their creativity in interpreting this year's theme of "Motion": this is what inspires us!

Manufactured by Amazon.ca
Bolton, ON

36200899R00098